LONG LIVE
THE POST HORN!

LONG LIVE
THE POST HORN!

A novel
by
Vigdis Hjorth

Translated
by Charlotte Barslund

VERSO

London • New York

This translation has been published with the financial support of NORLA

This English-language edition published by Verso 2020
Originally published as *Leve Posthornet!*
© Cappelen Damm AS 2013
Translation © Charlotte Barslund 2020

3 5 7 9 10 8 6 4 2

Verso
UK: 6 Meard Street, London W1F 0EG
US: 20 Jay Street, Suite 1010, Brooklyn, NY 11201
versobooks.com

Verso is the imprint of New Left Books

ISBN-13: 978-1-78873-313-7
ISBN-13: 978-1-78873-315-1 (US EBK)
ISBN-13: 978-1-78873-314-4 (UK EBK)

British Library Cataloguing in Publication Data
A catalogue record for this book is available from the British Library

Library of Congress Cataloging-in-Publication Data

Names: Hjorth, Vigdis, author. | Barslund, Charlotte, translator.
Title: Long live the post horn! / a novel by Vigdis Hjorth ; translated by
    Charlotte Barslund.
Other titles: Leve posthornet! English
Description: English-language edition. | London ; New York : Verso, 2020. |
    "Originally published as Leve Posthornet!"—Title page verso. | Summary:
    "A colleague's suicide prompts a media consultant to work with a postal
    workers' union struggling for survival. To her surprise, the new
    assignment brings hope at a time of personal desperation"— Provided by
    publisher.
Identifiers: LCCN 2020008295 (print) | LCCN 2020008296 (ebook) | ISBN
    9781788733137 (paperback) | ISBN 9781788733151 (US ebk) | ISBN
    9781788733144 (UK ebk)
Classification: LCC PT8951.18.J58 L4813 2020 (print) | LCC PT8951.18.J58
    (ebook) | DDC 839.823/74—dc23
LC record available at https://lccn.loc.gov/2020008295
LC ebook record available at https://lccn.loc.gov/2020008296

Typeset in Electra by Biblichor Ltd, Edinburgh
Printed and bound by CPI Group (UK) Ltd, Croydon, CR0 4YY

Long Live the Post Horn!

A NOVEL

Vigdis Hjorth

AUTHOR OF
WILL AND TESTAMENT

Long live the post horn! It's my instrument for many reasons, principally because you can never be sure to coax the same tone from it twice; a post horn is capable of producing an infinite number of possibilities, and he who puts his lips to it and invests his wisdom in it will never be guilty of repetition, and he who, instead of answering his friend, hands him a post horn for his amusement, says nothing yet explains everything. Praised be the post horn! It's my symbol. Just as the ascetics of old placed a skull on their desks for contemplation, so will the post horn on my desk always remind me of the meaning of life.

Constantin Constantius in *Repetition: A Venture in Experimental Psychology*, by Søren Kierkegaard

As I was putting away in my basement lock-up some sauce-pans that couldn't be used with my new induction hob, I came across an old diary from 2000. The diary had been a Christmas present and I had written in it for a few months before I got bored. As I hadn't thrown it away, might I have thought it contained something interesting I would want to read one day? I winced at the sight of it, but I still carried it upstairs and left it on the kitchen table. I did some ironing and continued to ignore it, but when I went to bed, I took it with me. I opened it and began reading; I had made entries almost every day from 1 January to 16 May. When I had finished, I felt so sickened I couldn't sleep. I got up and opened a window to let in some air. I drank some water and paced up and down the living room before I went back to bed and opened the diary again as if hoping something had changed. January's entries were about the winter sales and some guy named Per I thought might be interested in me. In February it was a guy called Tor and a Mulberry bag I'd managed to get half-price and a pair of shoes I should have bought half a size bigger. I appeared to have seen a lot of films I didn't like, spent time with female friends who bored me

1

and eaten a lot of rubbish. In between I had been to editorial meetings at *Romerikes Blad* and scribbled down my thoughts about people, but not once about issues; I had spent my Easter break somewhere hot so that when I came home I'd have a tan for this Tor who I didn't know if I liked, I couldn't remember him now, nor was he mentioned again after Easter. The names were interchangeable, as were the dates, there was no sense of progression, no coherence, no joy, only frustration; shopping, sunbathing, gossiping, eating – I might as well have written 'she' instead of 'I'. And had anything changed, had growing older made any difference?

I tried to recall the spring of 2000, but failed. I had lived through it, hadn't I? I had worked for *Romerikes Blad* where I covered sports events and local council meetings, only I couldn't remember a single sports event or council meeting; had I kept any of my articles? I ran back to the basement as if needing proof that these events really had taken place, but I no longer recognised the basement lock-up or the boxes, perhaps it wasn't my lock-up or my diary? I never found the articles, but came across some disconcertingly idiotic stuff which I was tempted to throw away or burn. Nevertheless I locked the door after me, walked back up the stairs to my flat and went to bed, but I still couldn't sleep. I'm coming down with something, I thought, I'm getting a temperature.

I dreamt my recurring dream where it's summer and I'm driving with the windows down and the wind in my hair, then

I glance up at the rear view mirror and see my mother sitting in the back, as if saying: Yes, here I am. I'm always with you!

The phone woke me up. It was Stein wondering where I was. I was supposed to meet him at noon in Norway Designs to help him choose a birthday present for his mother. I said I'd be there right away. I got up and I rushed because I felt bad about having forgotten about him and I knew the feeling would pass as soon as I got there, so I hurried so that it would pass, so that it too would soon be forgotten like all of 2000 and the years before that, so that soon everything would be shrouded in darkness as if it had never happened. Stein was waiting. How long had I known Stein? I couldn't remember when I first met him; I thought hard and fortunately it came back to me, Trond's fortieth birthday, almost a year ago, had I really been seeing Stein for almost a year now? Trond would be forty-one soon, one birthday after another, it was stored in my memory, all I had to do was retrieve it. Why was it so difficult and why did I need to remember what I had eaten, what I had bought, where I had parked the car, I parked in the multi-storey car park that was a part of the building where my office was and rushed down to the shop where he was waiting. We didn't kiss – perhaps he was annoyed that I was late. We settled on a glass vase from Kosta Boda, it was nice, I even considered buying one for myself before I remembered my diary. All the times I had gone to Norway Designs to buy birthday presents, all the times in the future when I would stand in front of the till in Norway Designs to pay for birthday presents. Stein thanked me for my help and I worked out how old he would have been in 2000, twenty-eight, what was he doing in 2000, I'd never asked him, would he remember if I did? He was running late and had to go. That's what we're like, I thought, always rushing. I could stop by my office, I thought, seeing that I was already in town and had paid for two hours' parking, then Margrete called and told me her period was late. I'm hoping I might be pregnant, she whispered as if someone might be eavesdropping. She asked if I would like to come for lunch tomorrow, Sunday lunch, she said, yes, I replied and walked down Stortingsgaten. I ought to feel a greater sense of awe, I thought. There was no substance in my diary. It was all about nothing. But that was my life and here I was. I decided not to go to the office after all, today was a Saturday, there was nothing that needed doing although it felt like it. My guilty conscience hadn't eased despite the Kosta Boda vase. Should I buy a new diary and write something else? Invent substance and key events or write an entry about the Kosta Boda vase, I really am coming down with something, I thought, so I drove home and went to bed to sleep it off.

When I got up the next morning, I felt better at first. I turned on my computer to begin an article for the next issue of ByggBo DIY magazine, but soon started to feel unwell. The components refused to turn into finished houses, the happy customers didn't seem happy, there was no joy in my language, perhaps there never had been? I opened old documents to find

4

a reassuring piece of earlier copy, but found nothing that wasn't lifeless. I turned off the computer; I really was sick. Even so I went to Margrete and Trond's where Mum had already arrived. Margrete opened the door and held a finger to her lips; it meant don't say anything about her period being late. We sat down to lunch as usual, to a meal worthy of a diary entry, I thought, roast lamb from Lom and organic potatoes. Nothing dramatic happened and yet my heart was racing. Should I ask them about 2000? I worked out how old Margrete was in 2000, twenty-three, she had yet to meet Trond. When did she meet Trond? I did know really, I just had to think about it. Why did I need to know? Because I wanted her to have a history. Because I wanted to have a history. There had to be a link between the past, the future and the present.

'Lamb from Lom is always so tasty,' Mum remarked; I visualised her in the back of my car, she hadn't changed. We agreed, as we always did, that the lamb was indeed delicious. Then we watched the seven o'clock news in silence and I drove home.

Monday morning I got up as usual, made coffee as usual, switched on my computer as usual, and was about to get back to ByggBo when Rolf rang, he sounded strange and asked me to come in. I asked what the matter was, he wouldn't say. I drove to work, he met me in the corridor, he looked grave, we went into my office. Rolf closed the door behind us and said that Dag had quit, then he handed me a piece of paper with Dag's characteristic handwriting:

Hi Rolf,

I've had enough, am taking my boat and going away indefinitely, might return to Norway, though not to Kraft-Kom, I'm giving up the PR business for good, never should have got into it in the first place, tell that spineless bitch we're in business with that I think everything she writes is shit, I've deleted everything on the computer so it's ready for the next poor sucker.

Dag

It had to be a joke. I looked up. Rolf shrugged. He said he'd called Dag repeatedly, but Dag's phone was switched off. He had called Dag's ex-wife, who said it was just like Dag to leave everyone in the lurch and do a runner. Rolf said that Dag had struggled to cope since his divorce. That Dag was having a breakdown. Rolf had driven to Dag's flat which looked abandoned, then down to Dag's boat, which was no longer moored in the marina.

'Is he serious?'

Rolf shrugged again. I looked at the note on the desk and gestured for him to leave, but he stayed where he was.

'Ellinor?' he said after a while and gulped. I flapped my hands again, he took a step back and said he would be in his office until five if I needed him. When his footsteps had faded away, I read the letter again. Had Dag been at the office last Friday? I checked my diary. No, he had said he would be working from home. Had he been in last Thursday? I tried to remember Thursday. After what seemed like forever I managed to recall Thursday, I thought I remembered him being at his desk when I left early in order to work from home, seeing his greying curls over the Mac and his glasses sliding down the bridge of his nose, but perhaps that was Wednesday? I hadn't spoken much to him recently, was that why? Or the stupid row we'd had about IT? Kraft-Kom hadn't turned out to be quite as lucrative as we had hoped, but even so? I tried to remember our last proper conversation, but it eluded me, he eluded me. I called Rolf to ask if he had seen this coming. He hesitated, which meant that yes, he had. I ought to be angry with him, I thought, but I couldn't manage it. I ought to despair or weep, but I couldn't manage that either. Would we be able to carry on without him? Keep calm, I thought, I went over to the window and asked myself what it meant in terms of the workload. Outside on the trees the yellowing leaves that had yet to fall were shaken by the wind, especially those near the top; it must be unnerving not to be able to choose your own ending, not to know which gust of wind will carry you off, not to be able to prepare for it.

I called Stein, but couldn't bring myself to tell him the news. I can't remember what I said. He was monosyllabic; I decided he probably had other things on his mind. I imagined Dag on his boat, at sea. I called Rolf again, he offered to come down to my office, but I said we could do it over the phone. What had Dag been working on? The postal directive. What postal directive? Someone would have to take over the postal directive.

'I'm on my way,' Rolf said and a moment later he appeared in my doorway. 'I can understand if you're upset,' he said.

'We have to do something if Dag really has quit.'

He sat down in one of the two chairs on the other side of my desk. We were silent for a long time. I didn't know what to say, I don't suppose he did either.

'Perhaps we should go home?' he said, his eyes were red. He misses Dag, I thought, he can't bear the thought of being here with just me.

'We have a lot of work to do,' I said.

'Surely we can take some time off to digest this?' he said.

I kept cool and asked if he thought we needed to replace Dag immediately. Was it true that Dag had deleted everything on his computer?

'Yes,' he said, 'and he has cleared out his office.'

At least I wouldn't have to go in there, I thought. We fell silent again. 'Spineless' and 'bitch' lingered in the air between us.

'And the postal directive?'

'The client is Postkom.'

I didn't know who or what Postkom was, but didn't want to ask.

'I attended some of the preliminary meetings,' Rolf said. 'I know what it's about, but it's a big job.'

I could see he was tired and I wanted him to leave, but if he left, what would I be left alone with?

'Why don't we sleep on it?' he said and got up. It's what people say when they don't know what else to do.

So he left and I was left alone. Finally something has happened, I thought, something I could have written about if I'd still kept a diary. But I wouldn't have been able to, I couldn't even react the way I was supposed to, the way Rolf did, with emotion, I just felt numb, my entry would have sounded as if this was just another thing I had eaten or bought.

I invited Stein home for dinner and luckily he had no other plans. While I cooked three courses, I listened to the radio. It calmed me down. I still couldn't tell him, Stein barely knew who Dag was anyway and perhaps it was Dag's idea of a joke. After dinner we went to bed and had sex. I didn't come so I faked it to reassure Stein, but he got up afterwards and said he'd rather sleep at his place. He had a morning meeting the next day and didn't want to be stuck in the rush-hour traffic on Mosseveien. I understood. He kissed me quickly and when the door had slammed shut after him and I heard his car start and drive off, I thought: He'll be gone soon. And then: Now he's in his car, thinking. I wonder what he's thinking about, I thought, but only for a moment, it was an exercise in futility. He was probably listening to the radio. I turned on the radio to hear what he was hearing, but there were too many channels. Did I feel pain anywhere? Near my heart perhaps? I fetched some paper from the printer, but couldn't find a pen anywhere. I nearly drove myself crazy looking for one. Finally I found one in a handbag and wrote my name on the paper, then I wanted to cross it out, but it felt like desperation.

Margrete rang and in an animated voice told me that she was pregnant, I wasn't as excited as I ought to have been, but it was late, I told her I had gone to bed.

The next morning we sat down in my office. Rolf had brought with him everything he had on the postal directive, which wasn't much. Dag had been working on it since April.

'So that's not the reason?'

'What?'

'Why he . . . quit?'

'No, no, it's the divorce!' he said. 'He'd had enough.'

'Sad that it should come to this,' he added.

He didn't think that Dag would come back; he was already factoring in Dag's absence.

'And the postal directive?' I said.

Rolf heaved a sigh and said we would have to ring the head of Postkom, that our priority now was to talk to the head of Postkom and get hold of the paperwork. He said he would do it, because he knew him.

He went out into the kitchen and came back with two cups of coffee, he set one down in front of me and stopped. I dreaded his putting his hand on my shoulder or touching me in some other way, but he returned to his chair, sat down, drank his coffee, took out his phone, found a number and raised the phone to his ear. Introduced himself and said that he had some bad news. He said that Dag Brodal had resigned with immediate effect and was currently abroad. Mentioned something about Dag's divorce and a breakdown, similar to what he told me yesterday. In conclusion he said that everything would be all right and that that was a promise.

He put down the phone and studied his hands in his lap before raising his eyebrows. 'We can't get out of it,' he said, 'the groundwork has been done, but they need someone to work on it until the Labour Party's annual conference in April. Early April,' he added. 'What are you working on at the moment?'

'I'm finishing off the next issue of ByggBo,' I said, 'but more importantly, I'm putting together the pitch for the Real Thing – that American chain of restaurants. You're the trade union expert.'

'I guess I'll have to do it then,' he sighed.

He left and I was troubled by the thought that there was just the two of us now, it had been better when we were three. React appropriately, I thought, be flexible, I thought, I opened a window to get some fresh air and tried to remember which month it was. October, of course, but it could have been March. Although the light is different in spring. This light was bright. There was something in the air. Perhaps I was allergic to it.

Stein turned up unannounced that evening. Or rather, he rang to ask if it was convenient to drop by. I was surprised, but I said OK, I wondered what he wanted, after all we had already paid for the tickets for our weekend break to London.

Had he heard about Dag? When he arrived, he was restless; he sat down in front of the television with the remote control, but found nothing that met with his approval. He asked if I had any wine, I went to the kitchen and opened a bottle while I waited for him to start talking. I thought: Well, he won't be driving home tonight.

We went to bed and had sex, he never said why he'd come over, he slept heavily or so it seemed to me. He put his arm around my back in his sleep, then it was as if he woke up and withdrew it. His breathing deepened once more. I looked at his face and thought that if I stared at it hard enough, he would wake up. But my staring didn't work. I tried to picture his body without clothes, but couldn't. It was only the man in the suit who appeared in my mind's eye. I wondered if he ever thought about me naked. I had no wish to snatch the duvet off him to see. I got up as quietly as I could, moving stealthily like a thief. In the hall I sat on the chair where he had left his clothes. Should I go through his pockets? I really am losing it, I thought. I'm going down the rabbit hole. There's no way out now, I thought. But if I don't scream, it's not happening to me. If I scream, it's over, I thought. But maybe it's over even if I don't scream, I thought.

I told myself to get a grip. My breathing settled down and I slipped back into bed as quietly as I had sneaked out. He hadn't noticed my absence.

~

When I woke up next morning, he was gone. I looked for a note but couldn't find one. I don't know why I had expected a note, and incidentally expected is too strong a word. Then again I didn't have a pen, I reminded myself. The one I found yesterday I had put in the kitchen drawer.

I worked on the issue of ByggBo all that week but didn't get very far. I sent what little I had to Rolf on the Thursday, so he could review it over the weekend and offer suggestions. He left the office early, he was going to his cabin and taking his boat, when he said the word 'boat' he ground to a halt, but didn't mention Dag. When I heard the sound of his car leaving, I printed out my draft and sat down in the chair by the window to read it. There were numerous typos. Tool had become fool, boss loss, light fright, power slower, I put down the pages and checked the computer, but there was nothing wrong with the word processing software. I was tempted to call Rolf and ask him not to open the document, but that would only make him want to. I wrote a restrained email saying I had accidentally sent him an old version and that the right one was on its way. I proofread the text again, there were even more errors than I had first noticed, and sent it to him an hour later.

As I was about to drive home, something weird happened. I turned on the ignition and the radio came on, loud music from P4, a station I never normally listen to. I switched it off, and it fell silent. The multi-storey car park was empty. I got the feeling that someone had been in my car. But who and why? Nothing was missing and yet I couldn't shake off this sense of an alien presence. Was it even my car? I looked for my gloves, they weren't there. I locked the doors. Had I even worn gloves that morning? I tried to recall my morning, but it was difficult, I'd had coffee and eggs for breakfast, or had I?

It was dark outside. The red and amber traffic lights seemed blurred. I need glasses, I thought, and was overcome by an urge to abandon the car, but that was impossible, of course. Dag didn't call. Was I expecting him to? Dag in a suit with files under his arm, walking up the stairs in the morning, walking down them in the afternoon, I tried to visualise him, curly greying hair over glasses, coat collar turned up against the wind, on his way to the point where he had had enough. I wanted to delete his number, but I couldn't find my phone. It wasn't in my handbag or on the passenger seat, had I left it behind? Would I have to drive back? Then it started to ring, it was on the floor in the back and I couldn't reach it without letting go of the steering wheel, it's Dag, I thought. I pulled over in a bus lay-by and managed to grab it, it was Rolf wanting to talk about the ByggBo text, I understood what he said. He had sent me an email about the postal directive, the meeting with the head of Postkom was scheduled for after the weekend.

I counted traffic lights for the rest of the drive, that helped. Once home I parked almost calmly and almost calmly went up the stairs and opened the door just as calmly. I made myself a cup of tea, sat down, then opened my email with some trepidation and breathed a sigh of relief. The EU's third postal directive was about allowing competition for letters weighing less than 50g. It didn't sound like a big deal. Kraft-Kom had been hired by Postkom, the Norwegian Post and Communications Union, to help them fight against its implementation. The first and second directive had been passed by Parliament with no objection, and the third one was bound to go through, also without objection, but we had to give them what they were paying us for.

I turned off my laptop and stared into the darkness. Who wouldn't rather be in the south? How long would it take to sail to the Mediterranean across ever warmer waters, then drop anchor by a Greek island, and live on what?

Letters weighing less than 50g. Dag had sat in his office next to mine with his head in his hands and his curls poking out between his fingers, having thrown in the towel as far as Kraft-Kom was concerned. Then he made a secret plan, he jumped ship and left us behind. One day he might even send us a 40g postcard with a picture of a woman in a bikini. Dag, you bastard, I thought.

London didn't disappoint. Stein and I had both been there before and knew where we were going. When we landed back at Gardermoen airport, it was noticeably cooler than when we left. We talked about going somewhere warm in the winter.

15

The darkness was the worst, we agreed. It won't be long now, Stein said. I could feel the cold in my flat when I let myself in.

The night before the meeting with the head of Postkom, I laid out the clothes I would be wearing the next day. When I woke up too early the next morning, I decided to wear something else. It troubled me that I couldn't trust last night's decision. It was so dark that it might as well be night. I checked the time repeatedly to make sure that it really was morning and I continued to have doubts, but the traffic was morning traffic. Cars moving slowly bumper to bumper, the drivers invisible in the darkness. It got into your bones, I could feel my mood darkening. I tried to think about the sunny destination Stein and I had talked about going to in January.

Rolf was wearing a camel-coloured coat, and so was I. Under his coat Rolf wore a grey suit, under my coat I wore a beige skirt and jacket. We walked through the centre of Oslo towards the rough side of town. The pavements were crowded, the people looked ill, the number of Romanian beggars multiplied, unemployed, dark-skinned immigrants hung around on street corners, every ten metres a junkie was selling the *Big Issue*. We'd never had a trade union client before. This is exciting, Rolf said. An inappropriate word, I thought. He asked how London had been, I couldn't find the appropriate adjective. The entrance to Postkom's offices in Møllergata number 10 was cold and dry. Rolf led the way, he'd been there before. Now all will be revealed, I thought. Dag, I thought.

Rolf knocked on the door and a voice called, 'Come in!' The man behind the desk got up, greeted us and led the way to a meeting room where coffee and sandwiches had been set out, but which no one touched during the short meeting. The man said he had enjoyed working with Dag and thought it strange that Dag had left the project, as every study they had commissioned had come to the conclusion they had been expecting it to reach, namely that implementing the directive was bound to lead to social dumping. He proceeded swiftly, as if we were already up to speed. Several trade unions had agreed resolutions opposing the directive. He was hoping the Trade Union Congress would also agree a resolution against the directive. The danger was that the Labour government might simply wave through the directive without debating it before the party's annual conference. We would need to work quietly with the party's grassroots and make sure that the issue was raised at the annual party conference in April. That was the plan. OK? Rolf made notes. Labour's local and county branches, he said, sliding two thick files across the desk, and asked Rolf to condense the most important information to an A4 fact sheet which could be distributed to trade union representatives. We would also need to hold a two-day media training course before Christmas. Rolf nodded. We got up and said goodbye. Back in the street, Rolf asked what I thought, I shook my head. Ah, well, he said.

Rolf had more meetings, so I walked back to the office on my own and sat down at my desk. It was growing dark, a mistake, surely? A thunderstorm was approaching. I saw it when I went over to the window and wondered whether I ought to unplug the computer. A charcoal sky was fast approaching and I felt a rush as I watched it. As if I welcomed the storm, then it passed, no thunder, instead it started to rain. The windscreen wipers on the slow-moving cars in the street below me struggled to keep the water at bay. I sat down again to start work on the pitch for the American restaurant chain, but to no avail. I didn't want to go home and decided to stay at the office overnight. I felt relieved once I had made the decision. I wanted Stein to call so I could tell him about it. I got up with renewed vigour, made tea, then thought that perhaps I ought to go home after all; there was nowhere to sleep at the office apart from the floor. I could do whatever I wanted, I told myself, and that was what made it so liberating. Exhausted I went home.

On Friday my writer's block lifted and I wrote a whole page of the Real Thing restaurant pitch, I wrote about all the things that were real and trendy these days, perhaps I've recovered, I thought. That evening I was due to visit Stein. He called in the early afternoon; when I saw his name, I thought: He's going to cancel. He postponed our date by one hour.

When I turned up, he hugged me almost solemnly. I had only been to his home a few times before because of his son. He was with his mother tonight, in the hall was a picture of a boy I presumed was him. A small, serious-looking boy on a tree stump in a forest. Stein had cooked a three-course meal. When we reached the coffee, he looked at me for a long time and said he had a present for me. It sounded odd, even he could feel it, I pressed the soles of my feet against the floor. He's nervous, I thought. He produced a square box from his jacket pocket. It contained a ring, I thanked him for it, and put it on my finger. What does it mean, I wondered, what's he saying, but I couldn't ask and I couldn't tell him about Dag either. So I told him that Margrete was pregnant, but regretted it immediately because what did that imply? He said he thought that was great news. We went to bed and had sex, using protection. I wished we had been at my place.

In the morning he drove me to Majorstukrysset so I could catch the Metro home; he was going to a football match with his son. I didn't catch the Metro home. I bought a latte and sat in a café reading old newspapers, I ought to buy today's papers, except they would be at the office, I thought about going there. Instead I walked towards the city centre. My new ring got caught in my knitted glove and I had to take off the glove to disentangle it. The new ring didn't match the ones I already had, I took off all my rings and put them back in new combinations, but the old ones had sat too long on the same fingers and wouldn't fit anywhere else. I was thinking about getting rid of all my old rings and just keeping the new one when I realised that I didn't know where I was, apart from near the city centre. I had veered left in order to avoid the streets with the most traffic. Around me neon advertising glowed and flashed in every colour, shapeless and hideously dressed people with strands of hair sticking out from under their hats and laden with bags were rushing in and out of shops, their faces grey. I aimed for Egertorget and the Metro station, the train for Bergkrystallen would be arriving in four intolerable minutes. Glum people in cheap clothes poured out of the carriages, unkempt and limping, clutching scruffy bags. Where were they going and why, dusty one-bedroom flats in cursory tower blocks filled with junk, crumbling houses between petrol stations and warehouses, pedestrian tunnels under train stations overflowing with rubbish, the unemployed, the undocumented. Obese people with crutches and hearing aids and sores on their faces, what kind of life was this? Being dumped here without ever having been asked, without wanting to, but to whom should I report my lack of interest, to whom should I complain?

I yearned for a breakdown. To surrender to it and be carted off to a quiet and balmy place far away where the pace was slow. The train arrived, I got on and moved as far into a corner as I could. An unknown woman touched my shoulder and said my name. We had been at primary school together, she declared, now she worked in the head office of the Post Office and had come across my name in a memo about a media training course. I said she must be mistaking me for someone else, got off the train too soon and walked through empty Saturday afternoon streets and saw blue screens glowing in the windows. There was a lid over the world. As in Sylvia Plath's *The Bell Jar*,

I thought. I wondered if I should read it again, but surely it would only intensify my sense of isolation, I punched my fists into the air as if to smash the glass, but nothing happened. Where are the others, I thought. If it's true, as it's claimed, that other people really exist. I'm swimming underwater, I thought. They scream and shout and carry on on TV, but what for? Anyone can work out that life is ultimately a losing game. Dag, I thought. The postal directive, I thought.

Once I got home, I turned on my laptop to work on the issue of ByggBo with Rolf's comments in mind, but that only made things worse. Sandals had become scandals, predecessor processor, idealist nihilist, exam amen. I tried to read the texts as if they hadn't been written by me and I didn't know what they were about, and they made no sense. I need to bin my old clothes, I thought, and buy new ones in different colours. I got rid of quite a lot, but not the most expensive pieces. At least I haven't lost my mind completely, I thought.

Stein called around ten o'clock that evening. I was surprised, but then again, he had given me a ring. I wondered if I should tell someone, but it didn't feel right. He asked if I fancied going for a walk tomorrow, which was a Sunday. But don't you have your son tomorrow, I said. He did, but said he wanted the three of us to go for a walk together.

I slept badly. When I got up and had showered, I realised that my outdoor clothes were at the bottom of the bag of clothes I was going to get rid of. I didn't want to have to take them out, but I had nothing else suitable, so I retrieved them, put them on, then took them off again. They lay on the floor and had managed to infect me, I had to shower again. So I put on a pair of jeans I had never worn before, and a jumper I hadn't worn either because it wasn't 'me', and a random jacket and got in my car. Margrete rang to tell me she had miscarried. She sobbed and was dreading telling Mum. I didn't know that she had told Mum about not getting her period, I tried to comfort her and said that she was bound to get pregnant again and decided not to say anything to Stein. His son would be there so it was the right call. I dreaded meeting his son. It was a long time since I had last spoken to a child. I dreaded it even more the closer I got, in the end I had to stop at a petrol station, go into the loo, sit down and lower my head to stop feeling dizzy. After several minutes I stood up, held my wrists under the cold tap and felt the cold rise up my arms. I tried not to look at myself in the mirror, but couldn't help it and was shocked by what I saw, I looked as if I had dressed up for a part. Someone tried the door handle to the cubicle I was in, if there had been a window I would have climbed out of it. Back in the car I called Stein and told him I didn't feel well. He asked what I meant, I had no reply. I'll have to think about it, I said. Aha, he said. I told him I would call back in five minutes. We're waiting by the kiosk, he said. As I got out of the car, I saw them by the kiosk just as he had said. Stein in hiking clothes with a small boy holding his hand. Stein's son. Should I say hi to the boy or shake his hand? I stuck my hand

22

far enough down for him to reach. He looked at it and at Stein, who nodded, then he held out his hand, it was limp and small. I said my name, he didn't say his. Stein said: This is Truls. Then we started walking, slowly, of course. Truls seemed subdued. I wondered if I should say something to lighten the mood, but what? Stein said they had taken part in a football match the day before, and I asked who had won.

'Truls scored lots of goals,' Stein said and smiled, they both smiled because he clearly hadn't. I didn't know how old Truls was and by now it was too late to ask. I knew that he was at school because Stein went to end-of-year celebrations. Stein was brave. My guess would be that Truls was in Year Two, but perhaps he was in Year One, I didn't know how big children were these days. The last stretch up to Ullevålseter where the slope was steep, everyone overtook us. Perhaps they thought I was the boy's mother, their faces seemed to suggest it. I felt an urge to say that I wasn't his mother. Everyone probably feels that way, I thought. Or else they could easily tell that I wasn't his real mother, that I was an outsider. That had to be it, the real mother would walk alongside them, the three of them would be together, I was the outsider. It was weird to think that he had been married before. He really has a bad habit of wanting to be married, I thought, and glanced at him without recognising him, I would have to break up with him. Once we reached Ullevålseter he bought waffles with strawberry jam for us all, he treated us, it was all too much. I said I needed to work that evening because I had a meeting about the postal directive the following day. I had hoped he would ask what the postal directive was, in order to work out what I would reply, but he didn't. He nodded and said that he understood. He needed to drive Truls to his mother's after dinner. Truls had decided what they would be having for dinner. So what are you going to have, I asked. Yes, what did you choose, Truls, Stein said, would you like to tell Ellinor? Truls would clearly prefer not to, but he didn't dare say so. Tacos, he said. So do you like tacos, I said, it was a stupid question to ask, obviously. And he didn't reply either. Stein stroked the boy's hair and I felt sorry for him, having to be with Stein the whole time. We got up, I put my costume back on and we headed back, on the way I got a text message from Rolf telling me he'd sent an email, so my saying I had to work wasn't a lie.

'That was a nice walk, Truls,' Stein said, before they got back in their car.

On the way home I stopped off to see Margrete and Trond. I had said that I would. When she opened the door, I could see that she'd been crying and I felt embarrassed. It doesn't matter, she said, and gave me a quick hug. I caught sight of my own face in the mirror behind her back and I, too, looked as if I'd been crying. My eyes were red and shiny. I felt like an imposter, a fraud, I blushed and in the mirror I saw myself blushing, and I bent down to unlace my boots. Luckily Margrete led the way in. Trond was sitting in front of his computer. He looked up and we nodded to each other. But of course it mattered. Margrete made green tea. As I drank it, I realised how good it tasted and thought that I ought to make myself green tea more often. Why did I so seldom drink green tea, given how good it was supposed to be for you? Then I felt guilty for having such thoughts and scared that Margrete might be able to guess them. She put out some carrot sticks as a snack, but I said I'd had waffles at Ullevålseter. I didn't mention Truls, now wasn't the time. Nor did I mention the ring. She said it hadn't been painful in a physical sense. She had just started bleeding. They had gone straight to casualty, but she had been bleeding too much, I wished she wouldn't talk so much about blood. She hadn't had to have dilation and curettage, everything had come out of its own accord, after all, it was early days. No, it hadn't hurt physically. But I could tell it had hurt mentally. I asked if she had told Mum, she shook her head. I'm dreading it, she said, I'll do it later, she said.

'You're bound to get pregnant again,' I said.

'While there's life, there's hope,' she said.

'Yes,' I said.

'But it's as if life is on hold,' she said.

When I left, I felt drained as if I had given everything I had to give. Squeezed, I thought, like a bag of wine you've wrung the last drops out of, a vacuum. If I had had a diary, I thought, what would I have written about? The trip to Ullevålseter and my visit to Margrete's, one event had succeeded the other, but they weren't connected. Apart from me being present in both of them, a peripheral, fossilised figure unsuited to being the protagonist, too weak to hold the fragments together.

25

Spineless, I thought, and became tearful and angry at Dag. Get a grip, I told myself sternly, and managed to get a grip, to keep a cool head, that's what it's about. I had work to do! Exactly! The meeting tomorrow morning was crucial. I made myself a pot of green tea and sat down in front of my laptop to read Rolf's email. By now it was dark outside, of course, but I sat in such a way that if anyone were to look up at my living room window from the street, they couldn't see me, only that the light was on, it helped to know that, I concentrated hard. Rolf wrote that Postkom feared that introducing competition on letter delivery would lead to pressure on their members' salaries and working conditions. So obviously they were concerned. But they also claimed that the directive would result in more expensive and worse postal services for most people as well as businesses, especially in the more remote parts of Norway beyond Oslo. This was the most important point to get across to the public and to Labour's grassroots. Labour was the key, he wrote. The other centre and centre-left parties would probably vote against it, but they didn't matter. However, if Labour agreed at their annual conference to use their right to object, then the Labour government would be forced to respect it.

In conclusion he wrote that Postkom was realistic when it came to changing people's minds and put their chances of success at less than five per cent. He, personally, felt they were even lower. If we won, he added in brackets, it would make history.

~

How to make the Labour Party do something. Why on earth would anyone have given us, given Dag, this particular assignment? Dag had been politically active on the left when he was young, but that was so long ago it was no longer relevant; right now out at sea somewhere he was laughing at us and the impossible task he had dumped on us. Dag, you bastard!

Rolf arrived in a grey suit. I wore a grey skirt and jacket. He had his camel coat over his suit, I had my camel coat over my suit, we held black briefcases in our hands. We looked as if we were dressed up to play a role. It troubled me and the feeling intensified. Our glossy leather briefcases looked as if they contained something important, as if we were going somewhere important. My strict suit signalling 'Here comes a businesswoman.' We strode with important faces through the filthy city. Our creative heads full of ideas which dull bureaucracy and trade unions couldn't do without, our priceless expertise, our slogan 'Kraft-Kom – Selling the Power of Thought'. Dressed impeccably by Steen & Strøm to instil trust and convince the client with our action plans in order to make a living, so that Rolf could put food on the table for his PR consultant kids. He drew attention to red bullet points on his PowerPoint presentation. He was well prepared. He was persuasive in a way. He didn't crack. Grassroots, he said with a kind of conviction. Elected representatives, he said. Union reps. He saved us. Our monthly pay cheque. If only they knew, I thought. It's just as well they don't, I thought. On our

27

way back, we agreed that we had put on a good show. A show, I thought. The client had got what they had paid for. There was no cheating. No one was tricking anyone. The participants seemed content. They had nodded in the places Rolf had expected them to nod. He smiled in his camel coat. I praised him. Why couldn't I just feel the way I used to? Except that was exactly what I didn't want.

As I walked past the shops after office hours, my eyes landed only on the things they would have landed on before, the things that had always attracted my attention. I thought about Dag who had made a radical choice. I wondered if I had a radical choice to make and was trying to imagine what it might be when Margrete rang to ask how we should celebrate Mum's seventieth birthday, which had totally slipped my mind. I said I was up for anything and that she was welcome to take charge because I knew she liked to organise. She sounded as if she had forgotten her miscarriage.

In my letter box I found an envelope and I recognised the handwriting, it was Dag's. I tore it open. He wrote that he regretted the note he had left on Rolf's desk, and which he presumed had come into my possession. 'Into my possession' was a strange expression coming from him. It was five short sentences on the back of a beer mat. He had gone over the top, but then I was used to him doing that, he wrote, adding a smiley. He apologised for the situation he had put Kraft-Kom in, but he had lost faith, he wrote. In what, I wondered. He didn't explain. The envelope was postmarked Cuxhaven, Deutschland. Frankly I preferred his tone in the note Rolf had shown me to these conciliatory phrases. He wished me all the best for the future, he wrote, but he had to be joking, surely.

When I arrived at the office the next day, Rolf wasn't there. That was unusual, it was ten o'clock in the morning. Occasionally he would be ill or absent for other reasons, but he would always let me know if he knew he wasn't going to be there. I didn't worry, I thought: This is worrying. At eleven thirty the front door sounded and moments later he appeared before me as white as the proverbial sheet. Dag is dead, he said. What, I said. Dag is dead, he said again. Drowned, he said, in the harbour basin in Calais. Where, I said. France, he said. They're not sure it was an accident, he said, they think he might have done it on purpose, killed himself, he said. It was strange to hear him use so strong an expression. He started to become visible again. What do you think, he said. I, I began and got no further, I, I said again, and managed to stutter: 'Words fail me.' I felt embarrassed at resorting to cliché at a time like this, but he nodded repeatedly as if to signal that he understood that I was stunned. I tried to feel the right feelings, react in the right way because he needed something, but I couldn't give it. We ought to share this, I thought, and yet I wanted him to leave and take his needs with him. He left immediately as if he had read my mind, a thought that alarmed me, what if he really could read my mind and had understood all the things he mustn't know, but before he closed the door, he said he needed some time on his own. I'll be back, he said, it sounded like a threat.

Dag dead, drowned? I couldn't believe it. I hadn't thought Dag had it in him. I hadn't seen such grandeur in Dag. I got up and went to Rolf's office, he was sitting at his desk, cradling his head in his hands, he looked up at me, his eyes filled with tears. He's reacting appropriately, I thought. But someone had to keep a cool head, I thought.

'What happened,' I asked, 'how did you find out and how do you know the information is reliable?'

That 'the information is reliable' was the wrong thing to say, I could tell. Again my thoughts wandered off and I didn't hear his reply. Please would you say it again, I asked him. I looked at his mouth and focussed on listening to the words, one after the other, the first, then the second, then the third, but when the fourth word came, I'd forgotten the first. Dag's ex-wife had called Rolf that morning. She had had a visit from a police officer and a clergyman because Dag's body had been found floating in the harbour basin in Calais. There were no signs of a struggle or any intoxication on his boat, everything was as it should have been, no evidence of a breakdown or disturbance. The weather had been fine. They hadn't found a note, but it might be on its way. The police were currently examining his computer and phone, the words were pouring out of him now, the post-mortem would confirm his impression that Dag had taken an overdose of sleeping tablets, which meant his death wasn't an accident. He expelled the words with a sob; I had never seen him like that.

'What are we going to do?' he said.

The room was swimming, the windows came towards me and opened up, there was a cold light outside that burned and beckoned me. Rolf was the stronger, I fell, I was lost. I tried to enter myself, hold myself together and I had to press my back against the chair to stop myself from running at the glass.

I don't remember how I got back to my own desk. Suddenly I was there and it felt as if I had just snapped out of something. I stood up to go to Rolf's office for an explanation. But you were there a moment ago, I said to myself. I listened out for him. Had he left? Had I asked him to leave? What time was it? I had taken off my wristwatch and put it somewhere. My mobile wasn't in my bag. The light outside was indeterminate; it might just as easily be late evening as early morning. I got up and tiptoed towards the door, opened it without making a sound and looked down the corridor, light was spilling out from under Rolf's door, he was there, so that was as it should be.

My phone was on the floor under my desk as if I had tripped and fallen. It was ten to three in the afternoon, I called Rolf and said I thought he should go home and take a few days off. He agreed. After all, you knew Dag best, I said, but maybe that wasn't true. I wanted him to leave, yet I dreaded him going and I wouldn't know what to do once he had gone, his footsteps down the stairs were heavy and echoing.

I couldn't work. I didn't want to go home. I couldn't go over to Stein's, it was Wednesday and he had his son. If Stein could have come over to my place, that might have been the answer. Dag is dead, I thought. I put on my coat and went out into the busy streets, intending to lose myself in the masses, it didn't work, I feared the masses, feared getting too close to them, the outstretched hands of the beggars and all the pickpockets, I clung to my possessions. My phone rang and I had to open my bag and find it quickly and someone would exploit my confusion and distraction and snatch it, I found it, it was Margrete calling. Dag is dead, I thought. She suggested giving Mum an alarm clock, the old one was broken. Is it? I said. Didn't you know, she said. Should I know? Should I visit more often, call Mum more often, are there rules for such things? I never wanted to visit or call her, but it's not about wanting to. An alarm clock, I thought, Margrete didn't think I was being suitably supportive. But listen, I felt like shouting. I wanted to be horrible: Have you forgotten your miscarriage? Why give Mum an alarm clock, what has she got to get up for, why can't she sleep and sleep until she dies!

The letter was postmarked Deutschland, I wrote as soon as I was safely at home with the pen from the kitchen drawer on a sheet of printer paper because I didn't have a diary or anything like that, a town in Germany or anywhere in the world, a tiny little place. The global postal service, I wrote, the first postman sprinting barefoot between Athens and Sparta to announce that the war was over. And before that from mountain top to mountain top, beacons with torches raised high and white smoke signals in the sky, and before that between distant historical civilisations and in the future between the galaxies. Sealed missives from continent to continent, from ocean to ocean, 'I'm alive' messages from across the Atlantic and Central Africa and death notices from Siberia and France and the fringes of China, from the front. The name of the addressee, my name written by a human hand, the hand of another living human being whose blood flowed through it. Fingers with curved, broad fingernails, clutching a pen, spelling out one letter after another, letters so closely linked to your identity that they can't be copied; write, I wrote, and I'll know who you are. A signature is like a fingerprint, unique and impossible to fake. Loops, lines, arches and dots, practically illegible and yet not. The rhythm of the line, the wave of the line, a decorative border framing blue ink and the image of you in another person's head, heart, hand, the idea of you in the mind of another as they write, vulnerable because what the writer is close to seeps out, the subconscious and repressed, it seeps out and makes itself known, the choice of words and the lightly trembling fingers writing on paper, not in sand, before it's too late and the human world is over, like the moment just before you drown, I wrote.

It felt as if I was granted a temporary reprieve from a harsh punishment as long as I carried on writing.

~

33

Rolf called Thursday afternoon, I was in the kitchen, Stein was coming for dinner. Dag's wife, he said. Dag's ex-wife, he said, had called. She and her new boyfriend found it awkward that she was still listed as Dag's next of kin. It meant having to escort the body home. She didn't want to do that. She had phoned Rolf to ask if he could do it. Travel with the coffin on the plane from Paris to Norway where Dag would be buried. Many practical matters follow in the wake of a death. Dag's parents were dead, I knew, and his children were young. He had a sister in Australia, but her husband was dying from cancer so she wouldn't be coming, I hadn't known that. He had been somewhat taken aback, Rolf said, but the ex-wife had argued that he was a close friend and colleague, and finally he had said yes. He asked if I would come with him.

After all it had been the three of us, he said. It had been the three of us for years, he said, both at *Romerikes Blad* and all the time it took us to get Kraft-Kom off the ground, he argued as she, the ex-wife, had probably argued. Even though it hasn't worked out exactly as we hoped, he added for his own part, even though business hasn't exactly been booming, he said, even though we haven't exactly become millionaires, even though we haven't been as close in the last two years as we were in the three first, he mumbled. After all, you organised us, he said in a louder voice, and I felt a prickling from my neck to my forehead like when I put too much wasabi on my sushi. I haven't forgotten the letter, he said, but he didn't mean it, not really, you know

Dag, you knew Dag, that's what Dag is like, what Dag was like.

Stein rang the entryphone, I buzzed him in, keen to finish the phone call before he reached my door. I'll think about it, I said. Great, Rolf said, as if that settled it.

Footsteps coming up the stairs. Steady and firm as if he knew where he was going. As if he was here on official business. I had the security chain on. He couldn't get in without my help. He didn't have a key. My girlfriends wanted their boyfriends to have a key. My girlfriends wanted to belong to their boyfriends in a way I couldn't belong to Stein. What was wrong with me? Was it because I didn't want to or couldn't or didn't I dare? To feel more grief than I felt. To feel more joy than I felt? The prospect repelled me more than it attracted me because I didn't want to believe in great joy. The doorbell rang, he was outside now, right next to me, perhaps he had rung the bell several times, there was something wrong with my ears. I unlocked the door, he smiled briefly and hugged me, then put his coat on a hanger. Will it help if I tell him everything, I wondered. But where to begin. How are things at the bank, I asked. He looked taken aback, had I never asked him about the bank? He did still work in a bank, didn't he? Am I lonely, I wondered. Is this diffuse feeling one of loneliness? Now he had said something about the bank, which I hadn't caught, he realised I hadn't and said it again. He had applied for another job within the bank and explained what it would involve. I pretended to understand. He asked how the

Postkom meeting had gone so I must have mentioned it to him. Now it was at the tip of my tongue. I felt the weight of it on my tongue. But it didn't come out. I was so tired. He asked if I had to get up early in the morning, no, I said. Me neither, he said. Then he asked if he could stay over? Of course, I said, and was about to add that after all he had put a ring on my finger, but I didn't want to joke about it. We went to bed and had sex. When it was over, he whispered in my ear that he was so pleased that I had met Truls and I was embarrassed on his behalf because he cared so much.

That night I imagined the coffin in the cargo hold of the plane in between suitcases and mailbags. And before it got there, Dag under a sheet in a hospital mortuary with a tag around his toe. Rumour has it this happens in real life just as it does in the movies. Identified, autopsied, lifted into a coffin and driven to the airport to be checked in. There are specific rules for repatriation, many people die abroad. Even more people die in places other than where they wish to be buried and where it's natural for them to be buried. I'm not the right person to talk about what's natural, I thought, I had never felt natural. But perhaps many others felt like me. Who could decide if my sense of what was unnatural was indeed natural or shared by many people? Who gets to decide what's natural, who is in charge here? But you yourself used the word, I stopped myself. Just now you claimed there were places where it was more natural to be buried than others, oh, you know what I mean, I shouted inside my head. Then I hushed myself

36

and ordered myself to calm down. This isn't getting you anywhere! But then how do I do it? How? Fight for something, came a whisper from the hallway.

I sat half up in bed. My heart was pounding. I would fly to France and accompany the coffin home. However, despite having made the decision, I didn't feel any less agitated, I wanted to make phone calls immediately, but it was the middle of the night and in the morning it would feel unreal and by the morning it felt unreal. The coffee machine gurgled, Stein yawned and stretched. We showered and got dressed. Then he suddenly had to rush. His bag was underneath the coats in the hall and didn't belong there. He stuffed everything into it and ran. I stood behind the curtains in the living room and watched him let himself into his car and drive off. What if he crashes and ends up in a wheelchair, I thought. And if I were to crash and end up in a wheelchair, would he look after me? It was impossible, everything was impossible, then last night's useless decision cropped up again. I called Rolf to tell him, but he didn't answer his phone, I kept calling, eager to speak to him before I changed my mind, I counted traffic lights, when I got to the fifth one, he picked up and I managed to say it. He said he would book the plane tickets immediately, and at the eighth junction I got a text message with a booking confirmation.

We flew Air France and it felt as if we were abroad the moment we stepped inside the cabin. It was past six o'clock in the evening and it had long grown dark outside. When they brought the drinks trolley, Rolf ordered a gin and tonic, he hadn't slept for two days. If only we'd had snow, he said, if only it had been white. I agreed, but saying it over and over felt wrong somehow. The embassy will know what to do, he declared, it was the kind of thing they did, they will probably be relieved we aren't the next of kin, he said, who would cry and carry on.

Before I knew it we had landed and there was plenty to deal with. Our luggage, the Metro, French street names and confusion about our room booking. We found the hotel and they were expecting us. After all, we're a team, Rolf said. We had a glass of wine in the lobby before going our separate ways. It was easier to be in another country.

The next morning we were picked up by an embassy car and driven to a hospital. At one point Rolf put his hand on mine, at the hospital reception he got dizzy and had to sit down. The ambassador was patient. Showed us to the hospital director's office where we were greeted gravely. The ambassador stayed behind, we followed the director to the lift down to the basement and along a corridor. We walked past several numbered blue doors until he stopped in front of a door marked 204, which was also blue, I noticed everything, I was calm and composed. The director unlocked the door and a chill wafted towards us as did the darkness until he switched on the light. A body lay under a green sheet on a trolley. The director walked to the end of the trolley where the body's head was and nodded for us to come closer. Which we did. The director drew the sheet to one side and we saw Dag's face, he looked at peace. His eyes were closed, someone had closed them. The director looked at us. We nodded, Rolf was calm, it was easier than we had thought. We left, the director switched off the light and locked the door, I felt sorry for Dag who had to remain behind. Then we took the lift up to the director's office where we signed to confirm that Dag was Dag. We were almost certain it was him. The ambassador showed us out to the waiting car. As it drove through the streets, the ambassador said that we didn't have to worry about a thing. The coffin would be collected by their hearse in Norway and taken to an undertakers they had an arrangement with.

Back outside the hotel we didn't know what to do with ourselves, so we decided to eat something though we weren't hungry. We wandered the streets at random and found a nice café. When we had sat down, Rolf ordered a gin and tonic, then he blushed and said he felt responsible. Was there anything we could have done, he wondered, I had a sense of déjà vu. It's completely unreal, he said, turning the menu over but he couldn't decide, so he ordered another gin and tonic and said that he had asked himself these last few days how well he really had known Dag. Perhaps we don't know one another, he said and looked at me. I was about to say that all men are islands. Then I remembered that it was the other way round, it goes 'no man is an island'. I couldn't think of anything to say in response which wasn't inadequate or trite. I had read about people who don't feel pain and are constantly at risk of injuring themselves as a result. Was I like that? Did things happen without me feeling them and would I suddenly one day be fatally wounded.

Rolf's wife rang. When he saw her name, his face lit up and he walked around the corner so I wouldn't hear. I wondered what she said that he needed so badly. It hadn't crossed my mind to call Stein, I hadn't even mentioned the trip to him, I told myself that if I tried to tell Stein about Dag, I would lose control, everything would pour out and he would see what I was really made of. I could send him a postcard, I thought. On the corner around which Rolf had gone was a newspaper kiosk, I went there and bought a postcard with a picture of the Eiffel Tower. I looked at Rolf, who stood with the mobile pressed against his ear, nodding earnestly as if hearing words of wisdom. I went back to the café table and wrote not Stein's but my own name and address in the address area and turned it over to write a message. Just then Rolf came back and said his wife would help with the practicalities, she had just buried an aunt and knew what needed doing.

We didn't notice the coffin on our way home. I looked for the hearse at Gardermoen airport, but didn't see one. Maybe they wait until all the passengers have left the plane, I thought, I continued to look for a hearse as we walked down

40

the long corridors whose windows faced the landing strip. They probably use ordinary cars; people are scared enough of flying as it is.

Once I got home, I didn't unpack. I didn't turn on the light. I sat down on a chair in the hallway and stayed there, still in my coat. I couldn't sleep, I couldn't work, but it wasn't bad enough yet, not ugly enough, I finally understood people who bash their heads against walls, I wanted concussion and blood. I dragged my suitcase down the three flights of stairs, got in the car and drove back to the airport. It grew dark as I drove, there will be snow soon. I bought a ticket for Paris, it was the only thing I could think of. I took the Metro from Charles de Gaulle to the same hotel as before, but it was fully booked. The receptionist got me a room in a hotel nearby and the cab drove too slowly for my liking, I felt impatient although there was nothing I had to do. My room was on the third floor, from the window I could see Notre-Dame and the Seine. When I looked across the street, I saw homeless people settle down for the night on a stretch of the pavement partly covered by an awning. They lined up close to one another on cardboard or newspapers, their possessions near their heads, in plastic bags, suitcases and trolleys. I couldn't take my eyes off them. They didn't talk to one another, but then again, perhaps I was too far away to hear, maybe they whispered. I wouldn't have dared, I would have been shy. They have no choice, I thought. They could have lain down further apart from one another, but the number of places protected from the elements was limited. Right below me, a man was sleeping in a telephone booth, his forehead resting against the panel above the telephone. He had wet himself. In the morning he was gone, they all were. As if they were never there. I had to stay another night. I called Rolf and told him I was ill. He understood. The funeral was this Friday, I would be well enough for that. When Stein called, I didn't answer my phone. I waited for night to fall. I sat in the window, then at a corner café, when the sun went down I went upstairs to put on warmer clothes before I went back out and crossed the street to the pavement where they had been lying. There was no trace of them. I could smell urine in the telephone booth. I looked at the people walking past. Old, well-dressed women with small dogs, men with scarves, a few young people rushing by, Japanese tourists. Where were the homeless now? In the parks, under the bridges, on benches designed so it's impossible to sleep on them I had read somewhere, but never thought about, not until now. Again I walked down the pavement where they had slept, unless my memory was playing tricks on me. It was getting dark, I walked along the river and when I turned around for the third time, I saw a shuffling figure dragging a shopping trolley. He made his way to the awning and carried on until the far end. Spread out some cardboard and placed a sleeping bag on top of it. It looked like he fell asleep instantly, he didn't move. His head was deep inside the sleeping bag. Whoever came next, number two, would lie down next to him. And she did. I tried to look busy, leaning my body forwards as if I was on my way somewhere. About a hundred metres past the sleeping area on the pavement, I stopped and waited, then I doubled back. Then there were three of them. The third alongside the second. Then a fourth alongside the third, only centimetres apart, not because they sought contact, not to keep warm, but to make room for as many people as possible, in order not to waste the space. Why didn't they keep one another company, I wondered. Why didn't they share a bottle of wine? Strum a guitar? Didn't they have a bottle of wine or a mouth organ? Look who's talking, I said to myself. Why don't you share a bottle of wine or strum a guitar? They were alone with their stories just like I was, I thought, except they were aware of it. They appeared to be together, they all seemed to be in the same boat, but they weren't. All they really had in common was that they had no place to sleep other than there, yet it was still something. Might I have had something in common with the other passengers on the train to Bergkrystallen? Could we have shared a bottle of wine as I made my way home that afternoon, had a singalong as we sat there on the Bergkrystallen train. The homeless under the awning didn't pretend to have something in common. Did people normally pretend to have something in common? I envied other people their togetherness, but was it fake, was there no such thing? How could I find out, who could address my suspicions? It grew dark, the streetlights were few, perhaps it was dangerous to be out now without being like them and yet still they had a kind of community, a community of which I was outside. There were no other living beings out now except for those who

43

were sleeping across the street, who looked like bundles of clothes or shrouded bodies, and more came shuffling and joined the ragged pile of bodies voluntarily, it looked like a war scene, it looked like disasters in Africa and the Balkans, the pile grew in front of my eyes, I had long since lost count, soon they took over, I grew so scared I couldn't breathe and I ran back to the hotel, I didn't turn on the light, I didn't undress but sat down by the window and continued to watch. At thirty minutes past midnight the man from last night staggered into the telephone booth, leaned his head against the panel above the telephone, his long arms dangling. At a quarter past one a dark stain grew on his trouser leg. This was the world. When I woke up, he was gone.

The scanty snow that had fallen while I'd been in Paris, whose light had made it easier for me to return, was rained off during the night, leaving the ground cold and grey. I dressed in black but put a red scarf and a pair of red gloves in the back of the car; I was going out for dinner with Stein that evening because it was Friday, because I didn't want him to come home to my place because I hadn't unpacked my suitcase and my flat smelled of distress.

The car park outside the chapel was half full. I wondered how many people would come to my funeral, then I cringed with embarrassment at my childishness. Dag's sons were bound to be there, I had seen pictures of them. Was having children the answer? For the second time in a short period, I had used the word 'answer' in connection with my situation. What's the situation, we would ask the clients who hired us, in order to produce a situation analysis where they would see themselves and go on to buy an expensive action plan. Was this a situation? Rolf and Heidi were standing by the door to the chapel, handing out a funeral order of service with a picture of Dag on the front. He was on his boat and wearing deck shoes, but it was too late to do anything about that now. I hugged Rolf and hugged Heidi and said I would like to have done more to help, but that I had been ill. They had ordered a wreath from Kraft-Kom with the words 'Thank you for everything', they hoped I thought it was OK. I thought it was OK, and I thanked them for everything they had done. I didn't know what else to say, it was like being abroad, I thought, when you don't understand what's going on. It struck me that I had always been abroad, I only knew abroad, where is my country, I wondered. Where do they speak my language, I asked myself and I was so wrapped up in my own thoughts that I didn't hear what Heidi said, she had been speaking for several minutes. I entered the chapel. The coffin was there after travelling all that way. Dag lay inside. I couldn't comprehend it. The first pews were almost full. A few people were scattered on the next ones, a single person sat right at the back. I entered the fifth pew to the right, and sat down second seat in from the aisle. From there I could see, but wasn't particularly noticeable. I thought I could see Dag's ex-wife, Tone, at the front with two restless boys on one side and on the other a tall, dark man, her new boyfriend. It wasn't up to me to decide if it was inappropriate. Rolf and Heidi came up the central aisle and sat at the end of the second row where they had reserved seats. Then a man dashed in at the last minute, sat down next to me, shook my hand and reminded me where we had met before, it was the head of Postkom. The doors were closed, I could tell from the light. A trumpet played something familiar. The vicar said something familiar, then it was time for us to sing, the dutiful among us hummed along. The vicar read from his notes and said that Dag had been a good father, a keen sailor and an enterprising PR consultant with the PR agency Kraft-Kom. He had also been a member of the goal team, he said, that had to be a mistake, he probably meant that Dag had been a goalie for his football team, something I knew he had been. But who knows, I thought about what Rolf had said about knowing one another. Again we mumbled along to something familiar and it was over. Tone and her sons left first, the dark man a half-step behind them, then some people I didn't know, distant family, school friends perhaps, then Rolf and Heidi and several strangers. Everyone lingered outside as if something might happen or needed doing. Then they left.

Rolf took the rest of the day off; as they made their way to the car Heidi put her arm around him, he looked like a beaten man.

The head of Postkom caught up with me in the car park and said that Dag's death was incredibly sad and unexpected. I didn't know if the information about the sleeping pills was common knowledge so I nodded mutely.

'But life must go on,' he said, and added that several people had signed up for our media training course.

'We continue the important work of fighting the postal directive,' he said, 'in Dag's spirit!'

He left and I wandered around among the gravestones although my feet were cold. Right now he was being cremated. I remembered Dag during my first summer working at *Romerikes Blad*. Dag's dreams and Dag's dark curls, Dag's gesturing arms and excited voice during morning meetings. Dag's grand visions and ideas aired during the first hopeful years after we had started Kraft-Kom. Dag's constant feeling of being on the brink, the very brink. But the big breakthrough never came, his hair turned grey. What kind of shame do you feel when you fail to realise your ambitions?

But so what? We're all going to die one day, what difference does a year or ten make when we'll be dead for such a long time, when our struggle is nothing but that of a fly caught in a spider's web which it hopes to escape only because it's still alive. While there's life, there's hope, Margrete had said, but hope for what? More life? If you're alive today, it's likely you'll be alive tomorrow, your death is postponed a little, and so when you're young you have great hope, as an adult it gets smaller and in old age even smaller, and on your deathbed it's a tiny, tiny hope, what kind of hope is it which depreciates with each hour? Why not emulate Dag? Why keep on going until I can't, why rush about with no goal or purpose, sated, tired, fed up with everything and yet still hungry, good for nothing, subjected to an existence I don't understand. Dag is dead, why? But why not? Even if you don't drown yourself, you'll still end up dead and so you might as well stop swimming today as tomorrow or the day after, except that the water was colder here than in France, and my feet were already cold. And yet there was something I couldn't dismiss with my logic; a restless yearning in my body like an unrequited love I couldn't get over.

I returned to my car and glanced at my red scarf and gloves on the back seat. Dinner at a restaurant with my boyfriend on a Friday night is nice, why couldn't I be excited about it? I tried getting excited about it, but to no avail, I turned on the radio, listened to a feature on a disastrous famine in the Horn of Africa, then turned the radio off. On Skovveien the Post Office logo caught my eye, I pulled in and parked illegally. The logo was a half red, half grey circle with a smaller white circle inside, it reminded me vaguely of the Chinese yin and yang symbol and it looked out of place in Skovveien. I went inside, it was a long time since I had last visited a post office. I didn't belong in there, and those who were there, customers queueing with their numbered tickets and the staff behind the counters didn't belong outside, in Skovveien, I wondered if they had a current account with the Post Office, people used to have that, I remembered. Then I rushed back outside in order not to get a parking ticket.

~

At the office I opened the pitch for the Real Thing. I had written thirteen sentences, my progress was so slow that I was still counting them. Dishes made from organic ingredients with a low carbon footprint; surely that was a good thing. Good for your health and good for the planet. An American chain of restaurants based exclusively on the real and authentic, why was it so hard to promote it? The sound of traffic in the street disappeared. I didn't believe in ghosts so who was in the corner whispering? Dag, I said out loud. Then it grew deathly quiet. I looked across the fjord where the fog was descending and spreading out, hiding the tops of tall buildings and the masts of the biggest boats, then the smaller ones until finally everything was covered in grey. It wasn't nature screaming, nature was cool and numb, remote and inaccessible, it was me screaming a non-scream, me who was in the process of evaporating from lack of sustenance, I was completely beside myself, yet I'd never been inside myself. How to make the leap from screaming to writing, I wrote. To achieve in my language something I couldn't achieve in my life, I wrote, then I got up, went to the toilet and looked in the mirror, I was ill, I had been out too late that night in Paris, if I had really been there, what did the homeless do when they fell ill? I've nudged you, someone whispered, now you'll have to fall and hurt yourself. Despair, the voice said.

I turned off the computer, I would need to go soon and felt impatience mixed with apprehension. I didn't know how to tell Stein about Dag and I'd have to, wouldn't I? If I couldn't tell my boyfriend about Dag, there was no hope for us. No hope at all, I thought. When I passed Dag's door on my way out, I opened it and switched on the light. The room was empty, of course. I sat down in his chair and took in the view. The same treetops as from my window, they were black now and immobile against the grey-brown sky. I waited for something to happen. A sign, orders or a physical reaction. I got up when the trees merged with the sky and was about to close the curtains when I noticed a memory stick on the windowsill.

The red scarf and gloves made no difference, I stood in front of the mirror and didn't know what to do with myself until I had to run in order not to be late for the dinner I had been dreading, only to find that Stein wasn't there yet. I hadn't imagined myself at the table, with him entering and spotting me. I had imagined him at the table and me entering in my scarf and gloves. He had chosen the restaurant and booked the table. I went to the café on the corner from where I could see the entrance to the restaurant. The waitress asked what I wanted and I didn't know. It was Friday and I had left the car at home, but even so was wine a good idea? I could barely keep my balance as it was, I was already walking on a tightrope, I had enough trouble focussing as it was, but ordering a Farris mineral water would be an admission that everything really was unravelling, that I was about to fall, but then again perhaps I had already fallen and was in freefall and so it didn't matter what I drank.

~

I ordered a beer and had just been served it when I spotted Stein. I had never observed him from a distance before. When we weren't together somewhere, we were out of sight of each other. He walked unevenly, straining as if he were thinking about how to lift his legs and put them down, as if he were concentrating. I decided to wait four minutes, then go down the street and into the restaurant and over to the table where he would be waiting just for me. He would smile and I would smile and I would stiffen as he smiled because he would see or smell my non-scream and run away screaming. I don't have to go, I thought, I can go home, fly to Paris and sleep under the awning. I walked down the street wearing my scarf and gloves. He smiled when he saw me, hugged me and said the scarf suited me. He was glad I was feeling better. He said he had gone skiing last night. He had driven to Sollihøgda, the snow had been OK, though there hadn't been much of it.

'I must admit,' he said. He made an admission about the snow. A strange way to put it. The wine arrived, I sipped it cautiously but felt nothing, perhaps it was all in my mind. I reminded myself that Dag was dead, reduced to ashes and that was as real as it could be. Stein talked about Truls. It must be nice to have a son, I could ask him about that, but he wouldn't understand the question. He would reply that it felt natural. As we left, he said: Your place or mine? Like they do on TV. But it was just a joke because we always went to my place. Yours, I said, and he grew distant for several minutes. He's going through his flat, I thought. He's wondering if there's anything incriminating lying about which I mustn't see. He had secrets, I realised, dark secrets, I could feel it, standing behind him in the lift. He started scanning the rooms as soon as he crossed the threshold. Without removing his shoes and before switching on the light, he went to the kitchen, picked up a letter from the table and stuffed it into his coat pocket. Then he turned on the tap, bent down and drank straight from it as if he was very thirsty, as if that explained why he had rushed into the darkness. If I hadn't been paying attention, I wouldn't have noticed the business with the letter. It was small and square, not rectangular like an official brown envelope. He returned to the hall, turned on the light, took off his shoes and hung his coat on a hanger. The letter didn't stick out of the pocket. I decided not to get up in the night and sneak into the hall to read it. I wanted to preserve the curiosity I felt at that moment. So I'm capable of feeling something, I thought, I touched his arm, he jumped. Was it a love letter? An old flame he couldn't forget who had suddenly got in touch? We didn't have sex, the letter had come between us.

When I woke up, he was in the kitchen with the newspaper and coffee. He had set the table for breakfast but hadn't wanted to start without me. We ate quickly, I said I had to go to the office. I had to buy Christmas presents, I had to look at Dag's memory stick, I still hadn't told him about Dag, why was it so hard to talk about Dag, what was wrong with me? He said he understood. I had to work, he had to work. But the bank is closed on a Saturday, I said, perhaps I sounded suspicious, I hadn't meant to. He said he had a key card to the bank, he had to finish off some papers, if I asked any more questions I'd never get out of here. We're just workhorses, he said. He didn't seem to have noticed anything different about me.

Saturday morning in Oslo in late November. Morose people with their heads bowed against the cold. Slush underneath my feet and oppressive sky above my head. My chest felt tight and there was a blinding, enervating light in the shops mixed with Hammond organ music everywhere. Rushing people, their eyes frantic, humiliated and wounded. The silence on the Metro and the chill, the sick and the fear of getting sick. Becoming like the people with whom I shared the city. I dissected the bodies coming towards me, found fault with their faces, I was repelled by the tiny lives they led and hated myself for my revulsion. Margrete called to ask what I wanted for Christmas, I wanted nothing but for my revulsion to diminish, I had pain where others had wishes and so I didn't answer. In the background I could hear the Sølvguttene choir singing carols, Margrete said she was trying to get into the Christmas spirit. I wasn't, I didn't even try, I was on autopilot. She ploughed on undeterred, asking more questions about Christmas, I thought we'd only just had Christmas, that I had only just helped Mum prepare the Christmas dinner, had only just put the big dishes we used for Christmas back in the cupboards and now I would have to take them out again? I never bothered changing the clock on the dashboard in my car because I would soon have to change it again, I didn't put my ski boots in the basement lock-up in the summer because it would soon be skiing weather again, and I'd only just filed my tax return when it was time to file it yet again. I felt exhausted, I wouldn't get my shopping done today, it would have to wait until tomorrow, the shops were open on Sundays. I imagined myself tomorrow in the same street, in the same slush, in the same darkness, I didn't suppose I would feel any better then than I did now so I might as well do my shopping today before it got too late so that I could sleep for as long as I wanted tomorrow morning, the whole day, not have to get up but carry on dreaming which was invariably more exciting than whatever would happen once I got up. Even during my worst nightmares I was more excited about continuing to dream than what the day I was waking up to would bring. There were dull, unimportant variations in my days, of course, but nothing major. The cars in front of and behind me in the traffic queue weren't the same every day, but such differences had no value, they weren't worth getting excited about.

I sat alone in the office with Dag's memory stick. It felt wrong, but necessary. There were only two files, named Postkom 1 and Postkom 2, the first was 75KB, the second 54KB, so nothing really. I opened the first file, dated 7 April 2009, the heading was Impossible:

Coffee now at Venstres Hus after meeting with Postkom: IMPORTANT.

1. Today it costs the same to post a letter in Finnmark as it does in Oslo. That's a good thing. If the Post Office were to face competition, it'll probably become more expensive to send a letter from Finnmark to Oslo than to send one within different parts of Oslo. That's a bad thing.

2. Were the Post Office to face competition, there is a risk that it would have no choice but to cut staff salaries and pensions. The number of full-time posts would go down, regular staff would be replaced by poorly paid casual workers without employment rights as has happened in Germany and the Netherlands. That's a bad thing.

3. The quality of Post Office services will drop because casual workers won't have the necessary skills. CHANCE WILL DECIDE IF YOUR LETTER ARRIVES.

That was it. I opened the second file dated 19 August 2010, so created more than a year after the first one and written only a few months ago. There was no heading and it was more disjointed:

At Venstres Hus after meeting with the PM's office. What can I say/write? Decisions that will have a huge impact on people's lives won't be made democratically because they are taken in rooms with an absence of critical thinking. IT'S IMPOSSIBLE TO DEAL WITH WHAT IS ACTUALLY HAPPENING.

Many blank lines, I didn't think there was anything more, then suddenly it said:

In life, as opposed to logic, there are contradictions which can't be cancelled out. When you have to *choose*.

Again, several blank lines, then just as suddenly:

This isn't irony. It's the end of irony. The arrow of grief is pulled out and I die.

I had never been this close to him. And he had never been as far from me. Choose between what? He had written in his note that he had lost faith, in what, in what?

The evening brought stars. I sat in my office chair for a long time gazing at them above the black treetops while I thought about Dag. The experienced old fox who had taken the young cub reporter under his wing. Trained her, me, and taken her, me, with him when he had the idea for Kraft-Kom. He had had great faith in Kraft-Kom and the firm had done well although not as well as expected, as we had hoped for, because Dag found it difficult to sell himself as it turned out, I had often thought so and had, on one occasion, hinted at it, I regretted that now. Dag's strange comments this past year, which I hadn't taken any notice of at the time, now seemed portentous: community, communicate, communism, comedy, tragedy, confusion.

I had realised the importance of everything that had been Dag just when everything that was Dag ended. With the benefit of hindsight, I grasped the magnitude of the loss. I went home to bed and wanted to dream, but never sank into the stage where dreams are shaped, and tomorrow's to-do list played on a loop behind my eyes. I could already feel the exhaustion I would feel in the morning because I had missed out on my dream sleep, it tensed my jaw. The stiffness in my back, my footsteps out of the bedroom, the cold floor, the stream into the lavatory and the water, my face in the mirror where all my ridiculous worries had embedded themselves into my forehead. Shower and shampoo in my hair, soap between my legs, under my arms, every morning, every morning. To get dressed and yet not suit myself. Wishing my wardrobe contained something else, to be surprised and then not be surprised, and yet not wear my best clothes in order not to wear them out. Save the best for later. For some day. My most expensive lingerie saved for something that would never happen, which I knew would never happen, which I didn't even hope would happen, and still I waited for the future, the future, for something which would never happen, for the world, such as it was, to change. Then it was morning and I got up to do what I had imagined, practically already lived. Thus I was able to live out the day before I actually lived it and get tired before the actual tiredness set in and not realise the significance of what was happening until afterwards, I was out of sync with myself.

The queue of traffic to the office, the multi-storey car park, the stairs up, the countless emails from Rolf about the media training course for Postkom, the impossible pitch for the Real Thing and the issue of ByggBo, which still wasn't ready. Reading my own words made me nauseous, they're choking me, I thought, I'm choking, I thought. The words were stolen, I'm selling stolen goods, they'll corrupt me, but I was already corrupt. Everything I thought, said and wrote was stolen and fraudulent. Not that I felt ashamed, I knew no shame, rather it was a feeling of claustrophobia because there were no other words with which I could think, talk, write, it pained me that I was lumbered with words that contaminated me, I was bogged down by what I had stolen and repeated ad nauseam and from which I couldn't escape, I'm heading for the edge, I thought. Dag, I thought.

Margrete called to remind me that today was Mum's birthday, I rang Mum to wish her a happy birthday. I asked if she was well. Yes, she said. I couldn't think of anything else to say, was that my fault and was it even right to talk about fault in this case? Margrete had probably spoken to Mum at great length, siblings are different. It's not a given that two sisters each have as much to talk to their mother about as the other does. Margrete and Mum had more in common than Mum

and I or Margrete and I. A capacity for uncomplicated com-
panionship, for instance. Would I like that ability? It would
make life simpler. Did Mum experience the same unease
following our brief conversation as I did? I thought she did,
but not to the same degree because she was disappointed in
me while I was disappointed in myself for being unable to do
what Margrete could. If I had had two mothers, I would have
been able to compare just like Mum, who had two daughters,
could compare. I arrived at Mum's in plenty of time and
waited in my car near the junction until I saw Margrete's car,
then I drove on so that we would get out of our cars at the
same time. She had brought a hamper. I thought about how
we had sat next to each other on the back seat of the car
during summer holidays when we were little, the times we
had fallen asleep on top of each other in the back seat. It was
something I knew rather than remembered. I tried to remember it rather than just know it, but couldn't do it. And now she
had said something I hadn't heard. She rang the doorbell and
the door was opened, we entered and walked up the stairs.
That's how it'll end, I thought. Alone in a one-bedroom flat
with vinyl flooring. Mum hugged us. It could be different, I
thought. Oh, you think so? Vinyl flooring for other people,
but not for you? I dreaded everything, I realised. Didn't I look
forward to anything at all? It's the present moment that
counts, I thought. The here and now. On Mum's sofa they
talked about the weather. Margrete asked about Mum's hip,
Mum said something about her hip. On the console table
there were pictures of us as children. Taken on a birthday

most likely. We had stiff bows in our hair. People didn't do bows anymore. I remembered a pale-yellow ribbon I had loved and felt a warm tingle. So the past was faintly alive inside me after all. You look tired, Mum said. Margrete took out the goodies from the hamper. Parma ham from Parma, Roquefort cheese from Roquefort, a loaf of bread, which was not only real and organic but made from spelt flour locally grown in Lommedalen, you couldn't get any closer to Stone Age bread than that. At this point I could have said something about the American restaurant chain, the Real Thing, but what, and Margrete had already produced a Christmas present, saying that Christmas was right around the corner. She said that every year on Mum's birthday because it fell at the start of December. She asked if Mum wanted us to come to hers for Christmas as we always did. She asked that every year. We were welcome to celebrate Christmas with her and Trond, she said, she said that every year. Mum said she preferred us to come to hers. At least for this year. She said that every year. I wondered if I was about to pass out. But she hoped that we could give her a hand with the food, Mum said. Of course, Margrete said. Every year. But one day it would end. It was certain that what happened every year would one day cease to happen. But then there would be something else which would happen every year for years to come. Such as Mum spending Christmas with Margrete and Trond rather than in her own home. She unwrapped the alarm clock and thanked us. She could use it to stop her napping too long in the afternoons. Because it made it hard to sleep at night. Then she had to take a sleeping pill and that was a bad thing. Margrete said it was easy to become addicted. I thought that could hardly matter. Mum said she would use the alarm clock to make sure she didn't oversleep and miss *Hotel Caesar*, something that had happened several times. What was the point of it all? Her spectacles lay on top of a half-solved crossword puzzle on the footstool in front of her armchair. Such a meagre existence. Would it never get bigger? Was I, too, condemned to this tiny life? Was that my future? I desperately hoped not, but then again I wasn't hoping for anything else, I had no ideas about anything different or larger, I foresaw nothing larger, but there had to be something! That was my problem, my stupidity that I couldn't reconcile myself to the little life as they could. They wanted nothing larger; they weren't tormented as I was by the lack of contact with something greater.

Rolf wore his camel coat and grey suit. We walked to Møllergata with our briefcases. I had emailed him to say that I thought the course plan looked OK to me. He was responsible for the first day and he was usually calm and organised, so why was I so nervous? Thirteen people were waiting for us in the big meeting room. They were leaning forwards as if something was at stake, as if we could help. The head of Postkom introduced us briefly, then we were on our own.

Rolf remained standing, I was supposed to sit down, but not with the audience facing him or next to him facing them, I grabbed a chair, dragged it to the window and sat down half facing them and half him.

'If the EU's third postal directive is implemented,' Rolf said, 'you risk losing your jobs.'

He wanted to turn up the heat, get them involved. I regretted sitting by the window, there was a draught.

'If the EU's third postal directive is implemented, the Post Office will be forced to compete in terms of salary and pension costs,' he said. 'Full-time employment contracts will probably be replaced by short-term ones.'

The union reps nodded fearfully. He went on listing other problems with the postal directive, which were quite a few, they nodded, they understood the seriousness of the situation and didn't want the EU's third postal directive to be implemented. I tried to put on my coat without causing a distraction.

'So how are we going to stop it?' Rolf said rhetorically.

'Yes, how?' one person said and I jumped. Rolf fell silent for a moment, then he resumed.

'You need to engage with the media,' he said, 'now that might sound strange and sinister to those of you who aren't used to dealing with the media, but there's a first time for everything!'

I forced my shoulders down, the media, the media, I thought about everything I'd written in the media, all my pointless drivel.

'And why is the media so important?' Rolf said and went on to quote from the crib sheet on power and democracy we tended to use, I could reel it off in my sleep.

'The media is a central arena for the allocation of resources,' he said, 'political, financial and social,' he said. 'It's about adapting to the media's narrative and the media want human interest, relatability, drama, conflict.'

He wrote the words on a whiteboard and asked them to make notes, and they made notes as if they were at school, as if we were their teachers, if only they knew, I thought, if only they'd read my diary from the spring of 2000 and realised who was sitting next to them in a tight skirt suit, soon the seams would burst and I would be standing naked on the square with a price tag around my neck. Rolf listed examples of human interest, relatability, drama and conflict from last week's papers. The horror, the horror!

'If you want to promote a cause today, it's crucial to be visible in the media.'

He chanted it like a mantra and he was right, that wasn't the problem, but we hadn't changed our tune in five years. He chanted it without thinking, as if the time for thinking, the time of insight was over, as if everything we needed to discover about life and society and the media had been discovered five years ago and since then it was just a question of going through the motions, we hadn't grown any wiser, we had stagnated, why hadn't I realised that until now?

'You need to become successful storytellers!' he chanted. 'Approach the media and the organisations you represent with captivating stories which they can relate to so your members in turn can tell the media, the voters and everybody else about the dangers of the postal directive, so it spreads like wildfire. Let the bush telegraph glow red-hot with stories about the menace of the EU's third postal directive!'

His face was red with fake passion and he loathed himself, a bootleg product; I found a painkiller in my bag but didn't have any water and couldn't leave, because I had to look at Rolf with fake interest.

'Make up worst-case scenarios and promote them to local papers, radio and TV channels! A media-savvy public expects other players to master reporting styles and exploit the specific media platforms they're seeking to influence.'

'But how?' the young man in the red T-shirt bearing the Post Office logo said again, not sarcastically, but with genuine interest, and it dawned on me that this really mattered to him. That to all of them this was serious, that hadn't occurred to me before and I blushed with shame, and Rolf looked at me and perhaps it dawned on him too. After a lengthy pause, he braced himself and tried again: 'Newspapers: call *Nordlys* and tell them how the hike in postal costs will cause businesses in Tromsø to go bust. Persuade local Labour politicians to speak out against the directive. Encourage politicians who are already against the directive to lobby their fellow party members; the same message from many people on many platforms, that's how you change people's *Weltanschauung*! Or, as we say in Norwegian, world view! Watch out for anything that could be linked to the postal directive. Seize the smallest scraps of information to make your case. Write letters to the newspapers in anticipation of Labour's county branches debating the directive prior to the party's annual conferences. Make sure that as many people as possible turn up at Labour's annual conference, having already pledged to support you. Every little helps. Work from the bottom up, starting with the grassroots. A journey of a thousand miles begins with a single step. Labour's top brass is the enemy! The TUC's General Secretary is the enemy! You may think they care about you, but they're faking it, trust me!'

He had done his homework. They sat up on hearing *Nordlys* and Tromsø. He distributed an A4 sheet with arguments against the postal directive and asked them to write letters to their respective local papers using it as a template, but stressed the importance of variation, of a personal touch. They bent over their Postkom notepads, holding the Postkom pens which had been put out.

I went to the loo, popped the painkiller into my mouth, drank water from the tap and prayed that none of the union reps would come in because I wouldn't know how to look at or talk to them. I smoothed my hair, put some lipstick on, then rubbed it off again. I wanted to take all my make-up off, but didn't have any make-up remover, what could I do not to look the way I did? I returned to the meeting room, they didn't seem to notice me, but when the time came for me to gather up the letters they had written, they would see me and then they would know. They wrote for dear life in order not to lose their jobs, their livelihoods, not to have their working conditions worsened, their pensions reduced. Half of them old and grey, the other half young with their tongues poking out of the corners of their mouths, postal workers with a common cause. I was lacking a cause, I realised, I wanted to sit in a room with people who feared what I feared, but what did I fear, now there was the rub! They handed back the sheets before they left, less burdened than when they had first arrived or so it seemed, perhaps writing helps after all? They were heading into town I gathered from their conversation, why was it out of the question that I might join them? I had work to do. I would be reading through their thirteen suggestions for letters to the editors against the postal directive in order to comment on them tomorrow.

'Was it OK?' Rolf wanted to know as we walked down the stairs.

'Totally,' I said, patting his shoulder. 'You'd done your homework,' I said, 'I liked the bit about the Labour top brass,' I said, 'and the TUC faking it.'

The postcard from Paris was waiting for me in my letter box just when I needed it, the ingenious postal system devised by human beings actually worked.

I pinned it on my noticeboard as a reminder of that. I had a cup of tea and got ready to start working, but kept putting it off. I took the union reps' letters out of my bag, put them on my desk, and still I procrastinated. I watched the news, then I really did have to get down to work. I hadn't read anything handwritten for a long time. Except my own handwriting on the postcard and Dag's on two occasions I didn't want to think about now. I tried to decipher the letters, what was this? Unable to believe my eyes and feeling very emotional, I put them down. Then I picked them up again to reassure myself that I hadn't been mistaken. What was it about them? It wasn't the individual words, the individual word, the individual sentence, the individual, limping sentences, but the feeling that rose from the paper, it had a presence, an immediacy as if what was written wasn't imagined but actually lived.

Had I had that ability once and lost it? Was I reading too much into them? I put the letters away, then took them out again; the feeling was less strong this time, but I wasn't mistaken. What would I say to Rolf? What would I say to the postal workers? They couldn't send these letters anywhere, they were useless. Did they know what they had done? They might lack my knowledge of how the media worked and what the media wanted and about power and democracy, but they had something else, something I didn't know how to describe and which they might lose if I taught them how the media worked, what the media wanted and about power and democracy. Was there a connection? If I taught them to do what I could do, coached them about the media, the language of politicians, the language of the powerful, the tools of the journalist, would they lose that something which I didn't know how to describe and couldn't articulate, something that felt like a punch to the stomach.

I had one job to do that night. When I woke up the next morning, I hadn't done it. I thought about calling Rolf and cancelling, but that would be running away like Dag. I thought about calling Rolf and saying that I wouldn't be able to talk about the 'contributions' and that we had to do something else, but that would be dumping the problem on him. I didn't get dressed in my skirt suit, what to wear? Doesn't matter, I said to myself, but it did matter, my outfit was wrong. So is it about style, I wondered, not substance? But I couldn't keep deliberating because time was passing and I mustn't be late. I put on a pair of trousers and a jumper, but Rolf would frown, so I took off my trousers, found a skirt instead, and drove off without looking at myself in the mirror and decided not to look at myself in the mirror for the rest of the day. I parked in the multi-storey car park and ran down Stortingsgaten past the Parliament building, up Grensen and onwards through the slush. Wet snow was falling, it melted in my hair and on my shoulders, my hair and shoulders got wet and my head and shoulders would be wet for hours now, I never carried a spare set of clothes in order not to spoil my appearance with a carrier bag. I still thought I could avoid getting wet though the snow that was falling was wet and I was thirty-five years old and ought to know by now that wet snow makes you wet, nor had I brought an umbrella. The Romanian beggars and piled-up snow on the pavement forced me into the road where there was churned-up filthy snow, which I had to walk through. It meant my feet got cold as well as wet, and I would find it difficult to concentrate as I always did when I was cold, something that was hard to avoid in Oslo in December, in the darkness and on this day, which was already bad enough as it was. I hadn't found an angle, I wasn't even close to a way in. Fortunately Rolf would be starting the course today. He was going to interview the union reps in front of a camera and afterwards show them the footage and comment on how they came across. I was dreading it, they were dreading it and would squirm, everyone would hate it and squirm in front of the cameraman, especially when he filmed them, and it would be unbearable to watch them squirm in their chairs faced with Rolf's endless repetitions now that I thought I knew them, having read their letters. We would teach them how to perform so they came across better on camera, me with my pounding heart would be teaching them to calm down.

Rolf had rearranged the room. At one end there was a platform, with two armchairs and a low table between them. At the other end chairs had been lined up in rows, just like in the cinema. Rolf was sitting in one of the armchairs on the platform while the photographer was focussing the camera on him. The union reps had yet to arrive. Perhaps they wouldn't come. That would suit us fine, I thought. Rolf leaned back, checked the notes he had written on small, square index cards like the ones they use on TV, then pointed to a chair in the far right-hand corner. I set down my bag on it and took off my coat, I was twitchy. The union reps turned up in clusters and sat down at the back.

'You're welcome to come closer,' Rolf said, but they didn't, they were no longer quite so obedient, they had realised that we couldn't help them, that we were faking it, just like Labour's top brass.

'If the letters to the newspapers you wrote yesterday are printed,' Rolf said, he was able to say that because he hadn't read them, 'and you're contacted by a radio or TV station, something that's not unlikely because you're union reps who have spoken up against power, then relax. Take a deep breath and think about what you're going to say.'

A deep breath would have been good advice if it hadn't come out of Rolf's mouth in the same old way. Take a deep breath, I told myself as if I hadn't heard it before and tried to follow my own advice, but I couldn't, my skirt was too tight.

'You don't have to rush even if the journalist is rushing you. You're absolutely entitled to take your time to think and speak calmly. You decide what you want to say and you say it. Don't let them knock you off balance! Don't let them get to you. Then repeat what you've decided to say and add nothing else. Articulate in advance what you want to say in three or four different ways, same content, different wrapping. Short and snappy. It's better you produce soundbites than the journalist does. Think about the cause, what you want to achieve, it's not your job to please the journalist or to impress the journalist. The journalist is a means, not an end.'

I knew what he meant. The journalist is a means, not an end. But the means can choose for which end it wants to be the means! Or can it?

He showed them some old video clips, an interview where the subject did badly and one where they did well.

'If you're invited to take part in a TV debate with someone who is in favour of the postal directive,' he said, pausing to prolong the tension, but they just looked at him blankly, 'then it's all about being prepared!' he said, 'and now we're going to prepare! Or rather, you're going to prepare,' he corrected himself.

There was no response and he lost his thread, normally our course participants would be squirming in their seats at this point, but the postal workers had had enough of our talk, they had worked out that we didn't know what was going on, not really, I knew that from their letters. The cameraman looked at his watch and Rolf asked who would like to go first. Still no reaction. He asked again with a slight quiver in his voice. Perhaps they heard it and took pity on him. A short, chubby, middle-aged woman got up, slowly made her way to the platform and sat down with her legs apart in the armchair opposite him. Rolf flicked through his cards and found the right question: 'And who are you?'

'I'm Asfrid Besso from Kirkenes,' the woman replied in a strong northern accent, pausing between every word, 'and I'm the union rep for the postal workers in Kirkenes. And I'm a proud member of a long line of postmen and women who carry their postbags through the harsh landscape of north-eastern Norway, who battle through storms on the tundra during the dark winters. My father was a postman and his father was a postman, my grandfather met wolves on his route and my father faced robbers on his route, but did they ever get his postbag? What do you think?'

Rolf was bamboozled, but my heartbeat changed pace and my breath filled my body.

'What do you think?' Asfrid said again, looking him straight in the eye. Rolf cleared his throat and asked more hesitantly: 'So are you against the EU's third postal directive?'

'What do you think?'

'It's not about what I think, I'm asking you what you think,' Rolf tried in a brusque voice, but it didn't work.

'So,' he added because the burden of proof now lay on him and not her, the audience could see that, 'what do you think about the postal directive, the third one so far?'

'Four, five, two, ten or three, directives, directors whatever, I don't care what you call them, why can't things just stay the way they are when the way they are works. Eh?'

'But doesn't the Post Office have to innovate and keep up with the times?'

He was reading aloud from his index card.

'Eh?' she said again.

'Should the Post Office stand in the way of progress?'

'What do you mean?'

'That the world is moving on and the Post Office has to move with it.'

'Are you sure the world is making progress?'

'Well . . .' he said, he would appear to mull it over.

'I was saying,' he tried again, reluctant to repeat himself and I felt sorry for him, but there was nothing I could do.

72

'Yes?'

'The world moves on,' Rolf said quickly and there was tittering as he tried to recover: 'What do you fear will happen if the directive is adopted?'

'What do you think?'

Rolf flicked frantically through his index cards, but failed to find what he was looking for; she looked at him like a queen gazing down on a subject.

'Is that what you're asking me, what I think will happen if the directive is passed?'

'Yes,' he said.

'Do you want my honest opinion?'

He nodded, but he looked increasingly unsure.

'The Russians will pour over the border illegally and do the job for a week or two for crap wages and no letters will be delivered because they don't know the language and can't read Norwegian and there'll be chaos and people will stop trusting the Post Office and stop sending important and heavy things through the post, and that'll be the end of the Post Office.'

Rolf paused at that point, he tried to catch my eye, but I looked away, I couldn't help him. The course participants had rallied, more raised their hands wanting to go next. Rolf pointed to an unassuming man in late middle age with serious glasses and a cardigan who swapped places with the plump woman.

'And what's your name?' Rolf asked, hoping for second time lucky.

'My name is Rudolf Karena Hansen,' the man said, 'and if you'll let me tell you what I think, then I'll tell you and you'll get to hear it.'

Rolf stiffened. Rudolf Karena Hansen turned his armchair to face the audience and the postal workers leaned forwards, clearly interested. Here it comes, I thought, this is how it begins.

'I', Rudolf Karena Hansen said, 'am a postman in the county of Finnmark, beyond the Arctic Circle. My route stretches from Bossekop to Eiby and covers 1,500 households, 3,303 people in total, and this spring there'll be 3,313 of us, if everything goes according to plan, which I hope it will. Every day I deliver the right letters and the right newspapers and the right parcels to the right people in the right place and at the right time. And during the last twenty-three years and nine months this job of mine has taught me a deep appreciation that although it's about delivering the right parcels to the right people at the right time and in the right place every day, six days a week, then this job also embodies the struggle between two different *Weltanschauungs*, or in other words and to put it bluntly, between the interests of the people and those of capitalism.'

Rolf jumped at the word. Rudolf Karena Hansen continued, unruffled by Rolf's shocked face, by my presence, still facing his colleagues who knew what he was talking about.

'This can be seen most clearly in the attitude to letters with unclear names or addresses, what we call "dead letters".'

There was nodding across the room.

'Any letter without a clear name or address is put in a box labelled "addressee unknown" or in a box on which the postmaster has written "address incomplete", unless the sender has written their address on the back in which case the letter is returned to sender, but this is rare. Letters with no sender are junked when the boxes are full.'

Again there was nodding in the back rows.

'Thrown in the bin with trash and junk mail and that day's big, fat, lying newspapers, lost for all time!'

Glum nodding ensued.

'But what if', Rudolf Karena Hansen said in a more solemn tone of voice, 'dead letters could be turned into living ones?'

'How?'

It was the young man wearing the T-shirt with the Post Office logo who was asking. Several people picked up their coats and bags and moved closer to the platform. Rolf looked pleadingly at me, but to no avail. Who needed to hear how to make something dead come alive more than I did?

Rudolf Karena Hansen raked his hand through his thin hair.

'One day,' he said with great dignity, 'a letter landed on my desk addressed to Helge Brun. There was no street or post code listed below the name, just the town of Alta. I didn't think there was a Helge Brun living in Alta, and indeed there wasn't. Of course I checked immediately whether there was a Helge Brun in any of the adjacent districts, there wasn't. There wasn't a single Helge Brun in the county of Finnmark. There were several Bruns across Norway, but Alta was written with such clear letters and so sure a hand and underlined that my intuition told me the letter must be intended for someone living in Alta. I looked up everyone in Alta whose first name was Helge, thinking that the surname might have been confused with a similar name; Brunsvik, Brunsgård, Brunæs, Bruk, Brøyn, Blå, Beige, but no, there was no Helge Blå in Alta or Finnmark. The letter had no sender, it was postmarked Drammen, but that was no use to me. After a week I said to myself: It's just an ordinary letter and I've spent enough time and energy trying to find out who it's for. So without a second thought, I sealed the letter's fate, wrote "addressee unknown" on it and put it in the appropriate box. However, two days later another letter to Helge Brun landed on my desk, again with an incomplete address, again postmarked Drammen. What should I do? I had already explored every avenue in vain. And so I also put this letter in the box marked "addressee unknown", but not before I had started to worry about my condemnations. Because I had a feeling that the sender knew the address was incomplete, but put their trust in the Post Office. And would the Post Office now let them down?'

No! I felt like shouting, but stopped myself. Rolf's hand with the square index cards hung awkwardly over the edge of the armchair, his mouth was slightly open, he's going to drop them, I thought. Rudolf Karena Hansen stroked his greying hair and we understood that he was a sorely tested man.

'After two sleepless weeks,' he said, 'I retrieved the letters from the death box, placed them on my desk and studied them. I concluded they had to be written by the same person.

I don't have to tell you how skilled postal workers are at deciphering human handwriting.'

'No!'

'And written by an old person, was my opinion. The hand wasn't unlike the hand of my late parents, slanting to the right and with the "t" looking like an "l" with a line across it. My reasoning was this: It's written by an old person, but not necessarily to an old person. An old person in Drammen, say, might be writing to a grandchild in Alta. However, the chances of a grandmother or grandfather not knowing in which street their grandchild lives are small, unless there's a deep family rift. A son or daughter who has broken contact with their parents and so the grandchildren don't see their grandparents for that reason, and the letter is a letter of reconciliation, a peace offering from a grandmother to a grandchild, perhaps. But if the name was wrong, it had to be another type of letter because grandparents will always know what their grandchildren are called, regardless of the circumstances. So I went through every possible and impossible scenario and came to the conclusion that it was probably an old person writing to another old person who, because they hadn't been in touch for years or decades even, took the chance to send their letter to Alta where Helge Brun had lived the last time she heard from or about him. I must admit I assumed the letter writer to be a woman, again I don't need to remind you of the intuition postal workers develop for which gender is behind the handwriting.'

'No!'

'A letter writer who trusted the Post Office to come to her rescue. Who took a chance and crossed her fingers. Minor details such as the lack of street name or house number didn't stop her writing, so urgent was her business, so great her faith in the Post Office. When there was no reply, she took another chance. Might it be a brave marriage proposal? Information about a child Helge Brun didn't know he had? The more I examined them, the more I became convinced that the letters were important. Postal workers have strong intuitions, I don't need to tell you that and as it happens, I was proved right.'

A buzz of excitement rippled through the room. Go on?

Rudolf Karena Hansen paused rhetorically. Rolf raised his hand, then looked at the postal workers and dropped it.

Their ears had pricked up, their eyes were shining, hanging on Rudolf Karena Hansen's every word, captivated by the tale of Helge Brun, identifying strongly with the narrator and his mysterious letters. Yesterday Rolf had told them to write down 'relatability' because the media wants something people can relate to, but what's the use of knowing what the media wants if you don't know the postal workers?

'From that moment on,' Rudolf Karena Hansen continued, 'I didn't just put letters into the right post boxes when I was out on my round. I knocked on doors and struck up conversations with any old people who were at home in the morning and children who were home alone after school and had time to chat to a trusted postman. I asked about Helge Brun and although no one could point me in his direction, it was the start of a fascinating period in my life. I heard many small stories which together made up a new and bigger story, the story of our district told from different points of view. Details and incidents I had never heard about, but which had had life-changing consequences for the individual and the community, I gained a better understanding of how people live together and how they depend on one another. Everything made sense and though my round now took twice as long as it used to, and the postmaster wondered at times what I was doing, I did everything I was supposed to and more, and in the evenings I sat in the office between piles of dead letters into which I tried to breathe life.'

It had grown even darker, but the starlight reached us and large snowflakes fell from the black sky in slow motion and didn't melt the moment they touched the street or someone's shoulder, but stayed and you could brush them off your shoulder and clear them from the street, but they would settle in the woods so that Stein could go skiing, and I imagined how the white snow was already lighting up the darkness in the Arctic where Rudolf Karena Hansen came from because everything is connected. Rolf had closed his eyes and Rudolf Karena Hansen continued:

'So one day I knocked on the door of Sture Sørensen, who lives at Sagveien 8 by the former sawmill, and the door was opened by a woman I hadn't met before. It was Sørensen's sister from the island of Sørøy. I was delivering the parish magazine and the National Home Owners Association magazine, we chatted about the weather, which is stormy at that time of year, and I added a question about Helge Brun. Sørensen's sister shook her head and said that if I'd asked about Helga Brun, that would have been another matter. Helga Brun, I repeated. It hadn't crossed my mind for one moment that I might have misread it, that the addressee might be a woman. I had become so fixated with the idea of a marriage proposal and an unknown child, I had identified so strongly with the sender that I never imagined she could be writing to a woman. To Helga Brun?'

Rudolf Karena Hansen held up a forefinger, raised his eyebrows and opened his mouth to illustrate his lightbulb moment. Rolf seized his chance, coughed and picked up an index card.

'And that's how I learned the story of Helga Brun,' Rudolf said swiftly.

'Aha?' the room exclaimed, we all wanted to hear about Helga Brun and Rolf lowered his arm.

'I spent the whole afternoon in the kitchen of the Sørensen siblings.'

'Go on?'

'Because it turned out, you see, that Helga Brun . . .'

'Yes?'

'Arrived on Sørøy one summer as a—'

'Why?'

The question came from the young man in the red Post Office T-shirt.

'Well, how can I explain,' Rudolf wondered out loud, and Rolf jumped in.

'I think we'll leave it there,' he said, but everyone wanted to know who Helga Brun was, what the letter said, and whether it was ever delivered. Rolf gave him one minute and looked at his watch.

'One minute?' Rudolf echoed, rolling his eyes at the camera. 'Helga received the letter on her deathbed, and it shone a completely new light on everything and lifted a burden from her shoulders so she could leave this life with her mind at peace. The sender, and yes, it was a woman, thanked Helga for what she had done on Sørøy in the summer of 1967 when Helga caused a scandal, when she was accused of having ruined the summer on Sørøy and forced to go back to Alta and told never to return. In the years that followed Helga had wondered, of course she had, if her behaviour could really have inflicted as much human damage as had been claimed at the time. She had only done what she believed to be right, but she was an honest person, and that's not always an advantage. And now a letter had arrived telling Helga how important her actions had been, not just for one person's life, but probably for many more.

'Who do you think you are? Helga Brun, the sheriff, the doctor and the vicar had asked when they seized her and marched her to the quay where they and the rest of the island's inhabitants were waiting for the boat, which would take her away.

'Who do you think you are?' Rudolf Karena Hansen said as if he was speaking to me although I was sitting where the room was darkest and hopefully out of sight.

81

'Well, who am I? Helga had replied, I often ask myself that question and I haven't found the answer yet; a full and final answer probably doesn't exist, but what I do know is, how I respond will determine my life. A timid answer will give me one life and a bold one another.

'With these telling words, Helga Brun left Sørøy,' Rudolf Karena Hansen concluded his tale.

'Right,' Rolf said, turning to us, to me, but Rudolf Karena Hansen hadn't finished yet: 'My point here', he said, 'is to show how important it is to turn dead letters into living ones. And that people are the decisive factor when that needs doing, and that's why postal workers must have job security, decent working conditions and enough time to dedicate themselves to this demanding and honourable job.'

Applause followed, Rudolf Karena Hansen got up, took a bow and savoured the ovation. Lunch arrived just as the clapping began to subside and Rolf looked desperately at the time. The postal workers made a beeline for the sandwiches and for Rudolf, no doubt hoping to ask him more about Helga Brun. Rolf dragged me out into the corridor.

'What do we do?'

I didn't know.

'I mean, somehow we're doing our job,' he said, 'aren't we?'

I didn't know.

'Delivering the media training course,' he said, 'which Postkom has approved and paid for?'

I didn't know.

'Delivering the media training course,' he repeated, muttering that it wasn't our fault if people didn't respond as they were supposed to.

I had no idea who I was or how to respond.

'I'm out of my depth here,' Rolf said and his lips quivered, 'what would Dag have done?'

Dag?

But Dag killed himself, I wanted to say. Dag ran away from the question, I wanted to say, but perhaps that wasn't what Dag had done, perhaps Dag had answered the question. But was his a timid response or a bold one? It couldn't be bold, I didn't want it to be bold! But at least he had made a choice, whereas I? I was a letter with an incomplete address, a letter with no contents.

'Shit,' Rolf said, sitting down on a windowsill and cradling his head in his hands.

I took a step back to look at him, but didn't see him, black and white dots were dancing in front of my eyes like on a damaged television.

'Shit,' he said again and rubbed his forehead hard, 'I need the money,' he said. Grey December, I thought. The darkness and the plummeting temperature.

'I'd like you to take over,' he said.

A union rep appeared and he jumped.

'I can't wait to see the film,' she said as she passed us.

'She can't wait to see the film,' he groaned once she was out of sight, 'they want to see it again, what are we going to do?' he said, 'what am I going to say? Can't you go through the letters to the editors,' he begged, 'please?'

Then his face paled and he looked up: 'What were they like?'

I imagined Rudolf Karena Hansen holding the letter for Helga Brun in his hands. Surrounded by scales, franking machines and staplers, stamps, pens, parcels and Post Office forms, piles of living letters that needed delivering to the right place at the right time, while he exercised his intelligence, knowledge and imagination on the dead ones. Extracted their secrets from them. He was absorbed in something meaningful, he belonged in a way I had never known, he was sustained by a decency I didn't have. His purpose was to give people what they wanted: living letters.

'I can take over,' I said, and Rolf instantly looked relieved, 'so that you can have some time out,' I said.

'Thank you,' he said, getting up. 'Thank you, thank you,' he said, 'I'll go rearrange the room,' he said.

I went to the loo, I held my hands under the hot tap for a long time, I counted to a hundred and looked in the mirror despite having vowed not to. Who do you think you are, I asked myself. Who are you and what's your purpose in life? What's your situation? This time it was me who was in need of a situation analysis and an action plan. The postal directive was a lost cause and it wouldn't hurt Kraft-Kom if Parliament passed this directive like it had passed all the others, no one would ever know how we had handled the media training course for Postkom. Or at least not many. To get a bad reputation was a risk for a PR firm, we might lose business and my job security might be jeopardised. But that applied to so many people, why would it be tougher for me than for the postal workers? Who profited from dead letters being turned into living ones? Financially it made no sense. Then again not everything can be measured in money. And what if profit was the most important criterion? What if people who got their once-dead-now-living letters became so happy they didn't buy anything for ages? Forget it, I thought, I left the loo, closing the door behind me, what else can you do when your house is on fire, I was freezing cold and burning hot at the same time.

They were clustered around Rudolf Karena Hansen and were undoubtedly asking him about Helga Brun. Rolf had rear-ranged the tables and chairs; he clapped his hands and asked them to sit down like they had yesterday and soon they were sitting with expectant faces in pairs at the rectangular tables as if in a classroom. Now it was my turn. I stood in the door way with my too tight skirt and wet feet, all I had to do was step forwards, but Rudolf Karena Hansen was a hard act to follow. Rolf had taken over my chair in the dark corner.

This isn't about you, I thought. You're just the means, I thought and took two small steps, but was still so near the wall that I could touch it.

'What can I say,' I stammered, aware that Rolf was twitch-ing, his face contorted on hearing my voice, which was thick, I could hear it myself, from emotion.

~

'I've read what you wrote yesterday,' I said, 'your letters to the editors,' I said, 'your draft letters,' I corrected myself, 'and I became', I said, but it was hard with Rolf looking so anxious in the background, I needed the wall, I supported myself against the wall and closed my eyes: 'I was', I said, '. . . moved.'

The word lingered in the air.

'It can be difficult', I said, still with my eyes closed, 'to understand why one text has the power to move us, while another leaves us cold. And what have I learned from being so moved by your letters? That I can't teach you how to communicate with the media,' I said, Rolf buried his head in his hands and pulled at what little hair he had left.

'If you were to write letters in the way I was going to teach you, your words wouldn't move anyone. I can't imagine many people would bother reading a contribution opposing the EU's third postal directive written from the template I was going to teach you. And which I'm now scrapping. I realised that when I read your letters yesterday,' I said, but it wasn't true, it was only now after listening to Asfrid Basso and Rudolf Karena Hansen that what had been opaque inside me had become clear. 'Maybe they're so different from what's published in the papers these days that no editor will consider printing them anyway. But I would argue that when you're up against the challenges we face in opposing the postal directive then the letters you wrote yesterday are a better avenue to pursue than my template. It's by going further down the route of your strangely moving letters that we might just win.'

~

An odd silence ensued and I needed the wall for support once more. Rolf was still sitting with his head in his hands, rocking back and forth.

'But what do we do?' Rudolf Karena Hansen said, and I wobbled despite the wall, shook my head, then turned my face to the wall with my shoulders shaking. Asfrid Basso came calmly up to me and whispered Sámi words in my ear. Rolf announced that the media training course should be regarded as finished. The participants packed up their things and left the room in silence, the last person to leave was Asfrid.

Once Rolf and I were alone, neither of us said anything for a while.

'I'm sorry,' I then whispered.

'It happens,' Rolf said, 'it has all been too much for us,' he said.

Another silence followed, then I said that I wanted to be alone. Rolf stood up with an effort and made to leave, he paused in the doorway and said for me to call if there was anything, I shook my head and apologised once more.

'Being human isn't easy,' he said, then he left, closing the door as quietly as possible, it sounded as if he tiptoed down the corridor to the lift, perhaps he was scared of bumping into the head of Postkom, who would ask about the training course and wonder why it had finished so early. Poor Rolf, I thought, it's worst just before you hit rock bottom. But it was coming up soon, I thought, and I couldn't do it for him. He had to hit rock bottom by himself. From the window I saw him go through the main entrance, his head bowed and bare, his shoulders hunched against the sleet and snow. He didn't turn left as I had expected, but walked straight into a bar.

My blood coursed quietly through me for a long time. In the corridor outside the footsteps grew fewer. The head of Postkom stopped by to ask how the media training course had gone, I said it had gone well and didn't elaborate. He said he would be in his office until late if I wanted him, he was working on an email exchange with the Aust-Agder branch of Young Labour. I didn't want something from him, I wanted something from myself. Only what was it?

It was time to go, but I was reluctant to step into the streets outside, to be in them as I had been in them before. For so long I'd been on some kind of merry-go-round that had finally stopped so I could get off and I didn't want to get back on. I was an empty vessel that had finally been filled with cargo, which had been sailing steadily wherever it was going but which now had to be unloaded. I couldn't find the right metaphor, but I was on to something and didn't want to go outside in the cold and the darkness and the streets filled with people, clusters of shabby, idle Somali men, throngs of people at bus and tram stops, the crowded square, big crates full of tat which people were reduced to buying because their lists were too long and money too tight, to be overwhelmed by despondency and loathing and rage at the trivial, pointless repetitions I couldn't escape, Christmas presents, the parking meter running out, red lights, my cold feet, which I had forgotten about, I remembered them now. I put on my coat and walked downstairs and outside, I stood in front of Møllergata 10 and took out a Christmas present list from my bag, the same one as last year and the year before that, there was no point in making a new one since Christmas came round the moment it was over. Dag, it said. Well, I could cross him out.

I walked down Møllergata and across Stortorget and onwards at random. I forced myself to breathe deeply into my stomach. Eventually my heart began to beat more calmly, it found a rhythm and stuck with it. My feet, too, found their own rhythm and eventually carried me up to Palace Park, there was joy in repetition. That Stein repeatedly got in touch with me, that Rolf kept going to the office so that I would see him on Monday. That Rolf's legs would most probably carry him up the stairs to the office on Monday even though I had let Kraft-Kom down and behaved unprofessionally. That my legs would carry me to the office on Monday so that I would see Rolf, that my heart would keep beating through the weekend to Monday just like the starry sky above me would keep on glowing in the darkness, just like the night would pass and the daylight would come, even in December, it never seemed to get bored with repeating itself for ever.

Unless something unexpected occurred! It could happen, I knew that now and I started dreading Monday. Monday and shopping for Christmas presents suddenly cast a shadow across Palace Park. I was spoiling today and the extraordinary time in Møllergata with thoughts of tomorrow and Christmas shopping and the other things I did reluctantly and from a sense of duty, I could torment myself with tomorrows and duties for a lifetime. But right now I had this unique day because today was happening right now and I guessed I could reconcile myself to it and be present in it, just like the ducks in the park seemed to be doing, they looked stuck frozen in the pond. And they seemed to be singing.

There was a post box on the building where the Narvesen kiosk was. There was one on the wall of the Hotel Bristol, I counted them all and it came to five post boxes in the short stretch to my car. They were red with the Post Office's slightly Oriental-looking logo and a promising opening. Once I got home, I opened my own small green letter box, it was empty today, but every now and then there was something in it. I made myself a cup of tea and took out the union rep letters to read them again, the strangest ones were written by the youngest people, judging by their handwriting.

My nan told me,
that postmen
rode red Harley-Davidson 1200cc with sidecars
in the tough thirties.
I wish
we could ride a Harley at work today,
but I hope times won't be tough.

Another concerned the night between 11 and 12 February 1830. It was a dark and stormy night judging by the text, perhaps you can judge by the text. The wind was lashing and postman Jørgen was freezing cold on his sledge going across Brunlaugslette in Fåberg. He carried precious letters from Trondheim in his bag. He was thinking about that and about what he wanted for Christmas, and what he would eat when he got home, tacos, and what he would drink, cola, and he was very much looking forward to it all, it said, and it made me think. Postman Jørgen was looking forward to crawling into a warm bed and to sleeping, but especially to waking up again, but right now Jørgen was fighting his way through the night. His ears were freezing as were the tips of his fingers, although he wore woollen mittens. READ TO THE END, it said in capitals. A sinister killer ambushed him from behind a boulder. Postman Jørgen was robbed and killed, there was a bloody and detailed description of his brutal murder. The blood trails led them to the postbag, it had been cut open, but the only thing missing was an envelope with lots of money for the Gudbrandsdalen Music Corps. Someone called Martin had done it, he was caught and sentenced to death and his head was chopped off. 'From then on that's when postmen were armed.'

I got up and started wandering around my flat. Looking forward to going to bed, sleeping and waking up again? And then be deprived of the experience because something unexpected happened. I googled the history of the Post Office

91

and found the incident described more matter-of-factly. The name of the murderer was Martin Pedersen and he was 'sentenced to losing his head and for his body to be broken on the wheel.' I googled 'broken on the wheel'. The cash that Martin Pedersen stole amounted to 365 speciedaler and 60 shillings. It was intended for the Gudbrandsdalen Musketeer Corps.

I could visualise it. The night, the killer and his victim. A justified fear. It was a true story. It had happened. And yet it was unimaginable. All the things that people have had to suffer, that people suffer. That I wouldn't have to suffer. I mustn't forget that or forget what others struggled with, or what those who had gone before me had struggled with, felt, thought, believed, and I must carry it with me. Familiarise myself with the past and reflect on the choices that had been made so that I could make better choices now and imagine the consequences of those choices for me, for others, for everyone, and in that way help create and take responsibility for the future of society.

There was comfort in this thought and it sustained me through the night.

Stein was picking me up around noon, we were going skiing. I was fetching the newspaper from the doormat when I heard the front door open downstairs. Was Stein early? He was normally bang on time. I leaned over the banister and saw the postman. I had never seen him before, it was because today was Saturday. He wheeled his cart into the stairwell. Bjerregaard, my upstairs neighbour, came out, I went back inside and closed my door. When I was sure that Bjerregaard would have gone back inside, I opened my door and listened out. The postman's jingling keys and the soft thuds of the letters. I thought about Stein's letter and Dag's letter and once, when I was little, letters from a pen pal in England, how much I'd looked forward to them! I went back inside and pressed my cheek against the door as I imagined my own letter box downstairs. Green and square with a keyhole and my name in black on white among all the others. Running down and putting the little key into the lock of my letter box, turning it and opening the little door, what would be waiting for me? I went to my laptop. Red post boxes and green letter boxes, I wrote, and the sound of the postman with his cart. The jingle of keys in the front door, the rumbling of the wheels on the marble floor, they ripple full of promise up the stairwell. The quivering silence while the postman flicks conscientiously and attentively through the letters, long live the postman! Who finds your letter and puts it in the right letter box. Love letters, birthday cards, postcards, invitations, certificates, passports and a much-awaited confirmation of an all clear after medical tests, blessed information from the council! Perhaps a bill, but we don't count them. The colour of post boxes, from now on my clothes will be red and green like those!

~

After the exclamation mark my thoughts reverted for a moment to last month's desire to reinvent myself. I had never owned a green garment and I couldn't imagine owning one now. The secretive gap of the letter box, I wrote. Too narrow for the biggest items, which must be collected with a delivery card, goods ordered online from the great abroad. Packaged and stamped, sent by courier, by car, whistling trains or planes and eased onto moving rubber and sorted by country, county, city and street and eased into the darkness of post-bags before being transported by the conveyor belt and the cart and the postman's decisive hands, every link equally vital. The postman's tireless wandering from stairwell to stairwell with the precious cargo. The steadfastness of the postman! Come rain or shine, the postman calls day after day, and the certainty of it, the predictability of the Post Office, the repetition! Long live the postman, the post box, the Post Office and all its beings!

I looked at what I'd written. It was useless, of course. But with something that felt like the elation I had just described, I rushed downstairs with the key. It fitted, that in itself was a miracle. There were two bills in my letter box. I'm not counting those, I said, parodying myself, smiling at myself.

We went to Ullevålseter. It was so busy that we couldn't walk side by side and talk. I felt the need to talk, so much had happened, but when I tried to decide how to start, I realised that I couldn't tell it in a way that made sense, after all, it didn't even make sense to me. Stein walked in front, I tried to get used to the sight of him. He existed, he was real, he had a heart. It pumped red blood through his body so that he could walk in front of me. The same applied to all the other people on the slope. But I found it difficult not to get irritated that there were so many of them, that they stopped and fell so it took forever before we could get our waffles with strawberry jam. The café was so crowded that we had to leave our skis all the way over by the toilets. Once inside I found two vacant chairs at the corner of a table and sat down on one and guarded the other, while Stein fetched coffee and waffles. A father and his daughter were sitting at the same table. I'm guessing they were father and daughter. The daughter was eating a waffle. Her father was staring into the fireplace, dreaming of another place. It's not easy being in the present, I thought. But perhaps they were, in their own way.

Stein didn't seem as bothered by the crowds as I was. It was so crowded that I couldn't ask if the crowds bothered him. I couldn't lean across the table and whisper into his ear. That would be rude. The queue for the till was long, but nobody jumped it. We ate our waffles. The man and his daughter got up and left, a family of four rushed up to secure their spot, placing their wet gloves and hats on the end of the table, hanging their steaming jackets on the back of the chairs and heading for the queue in their heavy, lumbering ski boots, shouting out orders and brushing sweaty strands of hair from one another's foreheads, wiping their noses with paper napkins, occupying space. I stuffed the last bite of my waffle covered with their germs into my mouth, inhaling them against my will, the slamming of doors jarred my ears, I had to get out of there. Then we left and didn't fall when we crossed the pistes. Once we reached the car, Stein asked if I wanted to come to his place for dinner. If I didn't have other plans, that is. I didn't have other plans as far as I could remember. He said he had a roast he could put in the oven. Then we could watch a film while it made itself comfortable, he said. I didn't like the phrase made itself comfortable. However, it might be nice to spend this dark evening with Stein. Seeing as Monday was some way off, I decided to be positive. I had a flashback to a roast in the oven after skiing. Something to do with my childhood. But that would have been on a Sunday, not a Saturday. I wondered if I was capable of being a part of a family. I thought Margrete had that ability. That she wanted to be a part of a family. I felt no such desire, but then again, I wouldn't know what that felt like. I had an inkling that being a part of a family was practical because most people had a family, because society was organised around the family, especially for holidays and religious festivals. So I would probably have my own family at some point like most people and start doing family things with my family in the same way I now did boyfriend things with my boyfriend. It was a depressing thought. That something life-changing would never happen. But what would it be? Children, I wondered, which Margrete so desperately wanted. Margrete might be pregnant, I thought, I suddenly felt that she was. That made me a little happier, the fact that I'd had an actual feeling except I couldn't call her to check if my hunch was correct because it probably wasn't. And then my calling would be hurtful or downright cruel. Besides, she probably wouldn't say anything until she was some months gone in view of what happened last time.

'What do you think?' Stein said.

Had he asked me a question and had I missed it?

'Are you listening?'

Perhaps I looked confused, he took my hand and said he thought I should come with him, so I came with him and stood next to him in the kitchen while he prepared the roast. I asked if I could help, but he had already peeled the potatoes and made a salad dressing, he had planned everything, and I wondered what he would have done if I'd said I had other plans. Then I would have had to tell him what they were and he would have had to eat the roast alone. I imagined him at the table alone with the roast and I felt sorry for him and wanted to pat his back except that he wasn't eating dinner on his own but standing by the sink next to me, and to pat his back would be wrong. Be present in the moment with yourself, I thought, be present in the moment with Stein, I thought; it turned out he had said something about the film we were going to watch, it was called *The Reader*. He asked if I wanted a glass of wine, and I threw caution to the wind and said yes. We sat next to each other on the sofa, each with our glass and watched the film while the roast was in the oven and soon a delicious aroma wafted across the room. Nothing unusual in that, of course. The film was about an unlikely pair of lovers before the Second World War. She is much older than him, but because she introduces the young man to the joys of sex, he is unable to tear himself away. He goes straight from school to the older woman and when they have made love, he reads aloud to her. Then the war comes, they are parted and don't meet again until it's over, in a courtroom where she is charged with being a guard at a concentration camp. He is in the public gallery. Time has passed, he has grown up so she doesn't recognise him. She is found guilty, but the boy realises during the trial that she is illiterate. It explains everything. Why she listened so intently when he read aloud to her before the war and why she was convicted of what she was convicted of, she didn't understand the papers that went through her hands. Only she doesn't want to admit it, so she accepts the verdict. Formulaic and sentimental, Holocaust in Hollywood, Kate Winslet as the woman, Stein was completely lost in it. He was the schoolboy who dreamed himself away between the woman's thighs, the boy racing his bicycle through the woods on his way to see her. He sighed along with him when they had sex, he was in the room with them, he would lean forwards when the tension rose, breathe more quickly, squeeze my arm when something sad happened, his face distraught, I could see it from the side. When everything was resolved at the end and the woman was somehow innocent and a victim and their love was somehow acceptable after all, Stein had tears in his eyes.

~

I told myself that he certainly wasn't a stone. He was capable of emotion. Whereas I was cold, stone cold? But I couldn't feel bad for not being moved by this film. Didn't he see it? How it exploited our longing for trials and tribulations, drama, meaning. He had seen the film before. Had he put it on to soften up the stone so that we could be moved together? To see if the stone could cry, but then it didn't, that in itself was certainly enough to make you cry. From his small and narrow world he longed for something greater, just like I did, and he watched the film to feel connected to history, just like I did with the postal workers, and believed himself to be closer to it by having seen the film. It tugged at his heartstrings and he felt himself transported from the hopeless world he couldn't influence until the film ended and the roast was ready and he was back in the miserable reality he had given up trying to change. A thousand miles away from his own being, just like me.

I remembered something he had said during our first dinner date, that he had always wondered whatever happened to his fairy tale. That had resonated with me. Because I, too, had been waiting for my fairy tale to begin, but I had waited in vain for so long that I had stopped believing in fairy tales. And it was my impression that he, too, had given up as far as fairy tales were concerned, and there was something familiar and comforting about that. Being with someone who believed in fairy tales would be too depressing because you knew that person was bound to be disappointed.

Then I was reminded of the letter, because we were eating at the kitchen table where it had been lying. So had his fairy tale found him after all in the form of a letter? A tale of unrequited love? His beloved had declared her love, but was tied to another and so he had to make do with me? Yet still he hoped? Had this been a Hollywood movie, I thought, and had the audience known the contents of the letter, they would pity him because he couldn't get the one he loved, but also pity me because I believed myself to be loved while my boyfriend loved another? Should I be pitied?

Towards the end of the meal he went to the hallway and came back with a square box wrapped in glossy black paper with a purple ribbon around.

'This is a shared present,' he said.

I unwrapped it with some trepidation, inside the box was a purple rubber gadget. He blushed when I took it out and asked him what it was for. He gave me the instructions, they were written in bad English and it took me a while to realise it was a sex toy. We had touched on the subject one evening some time ago, but I hadn't taken him seriously. He had asked if I had ever used a dildo and I had replied that not all modern women kept a dildo in their bedside drawer. I had spoken in jest, but perhaps he'd thought I really meant it. He hadn't followed it up, unless that was what he was doing now. I tried to keep a straight face, I was reminded of what Dag had written about irony. Stein said he had bought the most popular model online, the one with the highest ratings. I asked how it worked and he looked uncomfortable and seemed to think that I could figure it out for myself, as if I had experience of such things. An awkward silence ensued before he shrugged and reached for the wine, I returned the present to its box.

When we had gone to bed and were kissing and were about to have sex, he got up and went to the living room and returned with it. He tried to start it, it was supposed to vibrate, but he couldn't get it to work. He held it up against the lamp on the bedside table for a long time and I could see that the rubber was practically transparent. Then suddenly he got it going, it hummed and vibrated, he turned off the lamp, placed it between my legs and asked if it felt good.

'It's all right,' I said.

He held it up again, examined it and got it to vibrate at three different speeds, tried them on me, one after the other, and asked every time if it felt good, and every time I replied: 'It's all right.'

He inserted one vibrating end of the gadget inside me and put the other end near my clitoris, then he tried to get on top of me and enter me with the thingy still in place. He didn't say so using clean or dirty language, but I reckoned that was what he was trying to do, I might have been wrong, finally he got it to work so that it would also buzz for him and that was the point, I guessed. Is that good, he asked for the fifth time and for the fifth time I replied: 'It's all right.'

It took longer than usual for him to come, then he rolled over and took the gadget out of me, it continued to hum and vibrate, he tried to turn it off but couldn't, he held it up under the lamp on the bedside table again, the humming was louder now, he still wasn't able to turn it off, finally he got up and put it in the hall, but we could still hear it, he got up again and put it even further away, maybe in the kitchen drawer.

Do others feel the same way, I lay there wondering. Do other people have sex like this? I thought he had done it for my sake, I had a feeling he was doing it for my sake, that he wanted to be good enough, did he sense that I was missing something? Why didn't I just say no, why didn't I laugh, why didn't he laugh, why did we stay awkwardly not speaking, failing to find the words, silent in a rut we couldn't escape?

The letter, I thought, what kind of language might be found in a secret, possibly shameful letter? A direct and straightforward one as in the postal workers' letters, so far removed from mine and fascinating for that very reason. Perhaps I should sneak out of bed, read it and find out if he was embroiled in an unhappy love affair which wasn't ours. If his fairy tale had finally found him that would explain most things.

But, I thought, if an unrequited love story could be a fairy tale, then surely my unrequited love affair with life could be one too?

The next day we went skiing at Ullevålseter just as we had done the day before. We repeated our skiing trip. But it wasn't the same skiing trip. Sure, at first it felt just like it. There were

102

as many people on the slopes as the day before, as if all the people from the Saturday were also here on the Sunday, and they probably were. I tried to remember yesterday's trip, I relived yesterday's trip in my mind, and then imagined what would come next, the crowds at Ullevålseter and the waffles, I thought I could already taste them even though we'd only just reached Lake Sognsvann, but then Stein had a crash. On one of the last bends before the flat terrain and the lake, a heavy man smashed right into him. They fell over and Stein was unable to get up and put any weight on his foot, perhaps he had broken it. I didn't want to, but I had to call an ambulance. Many people gathered around us and heard my stammering. Half an hour later the ambulance arrived. While we waited for it, more people stopped to ask if we needed help, I told all of them that the ambulance was on its way. One woman gave me a jumper I could put under Stein, I made a note of her address and promised to send it back to her. It was embarrassing when the ambulance turned up and everybody had to get off the slope and people stared at us. Stein didn't say an awful lot, I'm guessing we speak less when we're in pain, I seem to remember that we do. We were taken to the hospital, Stein was wheeled in and I followed like his next of kin. There was a long, shabby, sad, impoverished, coughing queue of people. We should have asked them to take us to Volvat, the private hospital, but by then it was too late. The air was dense with germs, the lavatory stank, but I couldn't leave him now. Finally it was his turn, they X-rayed his foot. It was broken. He looked like he was thinking: I told you so. The ambulance would have been even more embarrassing if he had merely sprained it. They put his foot in plaster and the doctor said he would have to keep the plaster on for six weeks. Stein was annoyed, but bought a pair of crutches and we took a taxi back. I followed him upstairs and helped him get into bed. He had called his mother from the hospital and she was on her way. I left before she came. I had to get the car back.

The love letter, I wrote once I was back home, when it arrives with its declaration and everything is explained and out in the open. When it says black on white: I love you. I had never said those words, but now I had written them, bursting with unknown passion, with hitherto unknown hope. When the course has been set and the aim is clear, then no hesitation is necessary, I hammered away on the keyboard, my new secret love. No distractions in the form of responsibilities and unpaid bills, Christmas presents as yet unbought and time ticking away at the parking meter, forget all of that and remember this: that the button to be pushed is inside me and remember to push the button and climb the mountain of enlightenment and shout it out loud from the bottom of my heart, at that point I ran out of steam, but it was a start, wasn't it?

Rolf dropped out of our meeting with Postkom, he had trapped a nerve in his back and wouldn't be able to get to the office for days. I went to Møllergata on my own, feeling sick. What had the head of Postkom heard about the media training course, was he going to sack us? I counted the trees on my way there, they shook their heads as I walked past as if I disturbed their dignified presence with my racing heart, my overheating metabolism, my circulation, this whole noisy engine that was me, that creaked and jarred, there was a spanner in the works. I wore a red jumper as a peace offering, it was the first time I would be alone with the head of Postkom since the funeral. I knocked on his door with trepidation and he called out for me to enter, asked where Rolf was and I explained about the trapped nerve, he expressed his sympathy and led the way to the meeting room where the course had taken place, and I wondered whether the walls had ears and could speak, as they say. He asked me to take a seat, I took a seat, today again there was a plate on the table with sandwiches that neither of us touched. He didn't mention the course, he looked pleased, he leaned forwards eagerly and told me that the first objections against the directive were pouring in from local Labour Party branches.

'Or rather,' he corrected himself, 'we've received sixteen. But it's a start,' he said, 'and we still have three months to go, so it wouldn't surprise me if . . . well, upwards and onwards!' he said. He had travelled the length and breadth of the country these last few months, and met his own trade union members and local Labour Party members and county council members and Young Labour and couldn't help being, well, optimistic.

'But I'm aware that people like you aren't,' he said, 'you can't allow yourself to be,' he moderated himself, 'and ultimately that's probably a good thing,' he said, 'that some-body keeps their feet on the ground.'

But I didn't want to be that person. I wanted to be an opti-mist like him. Don't trouble trouble till trouble troubles you, I said to myself. Why worry about the day the directive was passed when I could enjoy the head of Postkom's joy that it hadn't yet been and might never be, or certainly not without protests and concessions. He said that although it had been exhausting to travel the length and breadth of the country, it had also been exhilarating because everyone agreed that it wasn't the postal workers or Labour Party members at grass-roots level who were the problem, but the party's leadership and the Brussels faithful elite who pushed all these directives through regardless. But still he hoped for a compromise. That opposition to the postal directive would be so significant that a few of Postkom's demands would be met, that, for example, they could get a derogation, other countries had managed to negotiate that. He assured me he always asked the postal workers not to focus on themselves as employees, but on the consequences for society as a whole. There will be poorer postal services for people and businesses, especially in the regions. We must not let the issue be seen as just another anti-EU campaign. And convince the public there would be no negative consequences for the EFTA agreement if the directive was voted down. He repeated himself, but he meant to. He repeated himself deliberately and with enthusiasm, that was the difference between his and my repetitions, which were neither intentional nor enthusiastic. Although strictly speaking there are no repetitions, it just feels like it when you're a human being living a human life. I had Stein's crash on the ski slope and Rolf's trapped nerve to remind me of that. The head of Postkom tossed me a pile of fact sheets and leaflets and said they had been distributed in their thousands and that he was working on more frequent contact with other union leaders in the TUC.

'But what do we do now,' he said, turning to me, 'given that we only have another 114 days left?'

I said I would put on my thinking cap. That I had a feeling I was close to a breakthrough. He wondered what it was, I said I needed time to articulate it.

'But trust me,' I said, infected by his exhilaration, we agreed to meet in the New Year.

Trust me, I had said, I was close to a breakthrough, for that was how it felt. He hadn't mentioned the media training course, perhaps the participants had felt so sorry for the sobbing PR consultant that they didn't want to rub salt into the wound by complaining to management. It wasn't a desperate thought. It was a heart-warming thought, the postal workers' hypothetical compassion warmed me as I walked down Møllergata, across Stortorget and the sun peeked out, quite unexpectedly, and I looked up at the sky where beautiful, newly formed clouds were drifting along, one looking like a glove, I decided I would get Stein a pair of gloves for Christmas! I tried to remember if Stein had a pair of gloves, I didn't think so, when we went to Ullevålseter he had been wearing mittens, I remembered that because I had looked after them along with the jumper from the other skier, I had forgotten about that, I must remember to send it back to her. But even if he already had a pair of gloves, it didn't matter if he got another pair, I myself owned many pairs. I went to the menswear section in Ferner Jacobsen and looked at several pairs of gloves. 'You can never have too many gloves,' I said to the shop assistant before feeling embarrassed at having said something so trite, but he didn't look as if he thought it was a stupid thing to say because he responded that yes indeed, people need gloves, a pair of gloves always makes a nice present, and I thought that a trivial remark could be true despite its banality. When we say Merry Christmas, we might genuinely want someone to have a merry Christmas, it's not the words that are important, but the feelings that accompany them. The shop assistant recommended a pair of black calf-skin gloves with stitching along the fingers and I bought them. While he gift-wrapped them, he told me about the time he'd lost a glove and got very upset because it was a fine and expensive pair bought abroad, from Harrods in London. He had looked for the lost glove for weeks without success and had finally thrown out the remaining one because what use was it when its fellow was missing, and would you believe it, the next day he found the first glove. That's not true, I thought, that's a story you've read somewhere. The shop assistant shook his head at the quirks of fate, he had found the first glove behind the hi-vis vest in his glove compartment, how on earth had it ended up there? He seemed sincere, he shared his strange tale with me, his customer, and I thought that perhaps it really had happened and perhaps I wasn't an unimportant person to him. Of course he had more important people in his life, his family and friends, but this was his workplace, selling men's clothing was his job, maybe he didn't sell black calfskin gloves every day, I looked around, there weren't many other shoppers in the department store although it was almost Christmas; I decided to respond.

'The story about your gloves almost sounds made up,' I said without any hint of irony, and he lit up and looked at me gratefully.

'Doesn't it just,' he said, 'it almost sounds made up,' he echoed pensively as proud as if I had given him a compliment and a present. So it was that easy. The gloves had been gift-wrapped and he put a heart-shaped sticker saying Merry Christmas on the box.

At home I found the bag from our trip to Ullevålseter, the jumper was at the bottom. I was ashamed I hadn't returned it yet, what had I been thinking? I had forgotten, I didn't think it was that important, it wasn't a particularly expensive jumper. What had I been thinking? Who was I to decide the value of the jumper? A woman had been kind and lent us her jumper, and here was I thinking it wasn't good enough? I found her number and texted her that I would send the jumper today, she thanked me. I drove to the post office in Holtet, but it had been closed, I drove to the post office in Nordstrand, which still existed and was different from what I remembered. They sold CDs and books and the queuing time was shorter than in the bank. I bought a big padded envelope and a CD with Christmas carols and drove home and looked at the jumper on the chair in the hall. An old, knitted jumper which looked out of place in my flat, perhaps it had been worn by generations, I thought, probably in an attempt to endow it with value. I tried but failed to recall the woman to whom it belonged. The memory was on my hard drive, I knew, it was stored somewhere in my mind and it was strange to think how much was on my hard drive, I didn't like the thought that other people could summon up a picture of me or recall my words, I had done and said so many foolish things, I had been careless with other people's jumpers. I picked it up and carried it to the dining table. I really ought to wash it, but wool takes a long time to dry and I had promised to send it today. And perhaps it might shrink in the wash and then I would be guilty of a greater crime. I bent down to sniff it and something incredible happened. I stared at the unfamiliar jumper on my dining table, then bent down and sniffed it again and again. It had her smell, I would swear to it, a unique human smell. Not repulsive, as I had feared. What if I, too, had a smell that lingered in my clothes and which those closest to me could recognise, yes, that's why I had sniffed the jumper again to have my insight confirmed. I had a smell and I could be identified by my smell and I couldn't hide no matter what words I used. A smell is a silent sign of far-reaching importance, I understood, had the postal workers sniffed me out from the very first day and realised everything?

~

I folded the jumper as neatly as I could, placed it in the padded envelope with a thank-you card, the Christmas carol CD and a picture of Stein on his crutches, and drove back to the post office. The queue was longer this time, Christmas presents being sent to Berlevåg, Bodø, Bergen and Belgium because people want to be kind to one another at Christmas. I tried not to be impatient, besides I could bill this hour as research because you can't work on the postal directive without knowledge of a post office. When the envelope had been sent as registered post to Tåsen, my mind was easier than before despite my olfactory epiphany earlier that day. Because all insights are useful, I thought, and in order for me to make the best possible choices, I had to understand how things actually worked. The kind skier with the unique scent would get the envelope the day after tomorrow, the post office clerk had assured me, and I imagined how she would open it and be delighted at the sight of her jumper and surprised at the music and the thank-you card and conclude that people could be trusted.

Outside the post office I watched the inky sky fill with stars and a glossy, smiling moon appear above the snowy spruces. It's like a postcard, I thought, not banal, just improbable.

You must answer boldly, I reminded myself.

Christmas repeated itself. Stein's mother had moved in and was looking after him. I stopped by just before Christmas with the gloves. She greeted me briefly, I had met her once before.

Truls was sitting on the living room floor with a toy car and didn't look up. I wondered if I should have bought him a present as well, I had completely forgotten about him. But Stein didn't have a present for me; he said he would get me one when he was fully recovered. Then again he couldn't very well ask his mother to go to the sex shop, could he, I thought, but then felt cross with myself because I was making fun of Stein, who only wanted to do what was best. And given that Stein hadn't got me a present, it didn't really matter that I hadn't got one for Truls, but then it hit me that the two were completely unrelated. Truls was just a child, I reminded myself, and was ashamed it had taken me this long to recognise that.

On Christmas Eve I went to Mum's around two in the afternoon. Margrete was already there. We did the things we usually did. Margrete had made organic sauerkraut with a small carbon footprint, and red cabbage from scratch and peeled potatoes. I cut up the organic fruit, which was entirely authentic and had a small carbon footprint as well. When 'Fairest Lord Jesus' could be heard on the CD player, Margrete started to cry. She didn't make a sound, but the tears trickled down her cheeks and landed on the pork roast. I only noticed them because I happened to glance at her sidelong. Or maybe it wasn't by chance. I got the feeling she didn't want me to say anything. When Trond turned up, he hugged her in a strange way. There was something they weren't telling us. Mum asked how Stein was. I said that his mother had moved in with him for the time being. She nodded as if that was a good idea. We sat down for dinner at four o'clock. Trond asked me about work. Was this the moment? I mentioned the postal directive, but they didn't seem terribly interested. Nor did they comment on the fruit salad when we finally ate it. I had followed the recipe, but it didn't taste as expected. I always follow the recipe, I thought, I go by the book in most things, but it didn't taste as I'd expected. Then again, I thought, nobody had ever promised me anything about the taste of the fruit salad or anything else. But it felt as if I had been promised that if I followed the recipe, I would be rewarded. And then it didn't taste as I'd expected, it had no smell, it had hardly any taste at all. Were there other recipes, online perhaps? Yet again I had missed out on the conversation though I could bet it had been about Mum's hip. Don't be such a bitch, I checked myself, no more irony. I ordered myself, that's enough sarcasm now! I didn't want to distance myself, I wanted to engage with the present, but how could I without faking it. Stop faking, I ordered myself, be real! We watched *National Lampoon's Christmas Vacation* on the TV but no one laughed, and it struck me that I hadn't had a proper childhood, I'd never experienced the spontaneity that the children in the film displayed. But then again it's just a movie, I reminded myself, a silly Hollywood movie made to entertain, it's not meant to be real. I had flashbacks to Truls walking up to Ullevålseter, eating the sickly-sweet waffles in the café there and playing on the floor of Stein's living room, and I felt sorry for him because he lacked it too, this spontaneity the little skiers had, kids who ran about, laughed, fell over, whooped and wiped damp hair away from each other's foreheads, they had got on my nerves with their noises and their vivacity, and I realised with a jolt that I was seeing my younger self, an awkward, introverted child, in Truls. We cleared up, then returned to the sofa with coffee and all the biscuits that Mum had baked. And now what? When Trond opened his present from his parents, a sheath knife with a carved bone handle, Mum's face changed and she said that it was just like the one Harald had, then she closed her mouth and turned bright red. It was the first time I had heard her say Dad's name since his death. An awkward silence fell. Trond said he'd given his parents a bottle of fine champagne and wrapped in a shoebox so they wouldn't know what it was, but when he spoke to them just now, they told him that their neighbour had stopped by with two bottles of fine champagne.

'All good things come in threes,' Margrete said.

My mobile rang, it was Stein thanking me for the gloves and I walked away so they wouldn't hear what I said, the words I used, the way I spoke to him, I hadn't made much progress, I was just as inadequate as I always had been. We told each other what we had been given for Christmas, it wasn't much, I asked him to say hi to Truls. Eh, he said. Say hi to Truls, I said again and added that I had a present for Truls, which I had forgotten to bring, which was kind of true. Trond had a brandy, Margrete wasn't drinking, obviously. I took my new bath towels and drove home around nine o'clock.

~

Once I got home, I opened my laptop to begin writing the Real Thing pitch, not because I wanted to but because I had to, to get it over and done with so I could devote myself to the postal directive. I wrote that the Real Thing was likely to be a success. There was a big market for all things real and genuine since many people felt themselves to be fake and imposters, I wrote, myself included, I added, but deleted it, it might be heartfelt and true but it was unprofessional. Then I hit a wall. What exactly did 'real' mean? Margrete would often use the word 'real' when talking about food. Certain vegetables were more real than others, organic ones that hadn't been sprayed with chemicals and those grown without the use of artificial fertiliser. GM sweetcorn was by definition less real than regular sweetcorn, but had regular sweetcorn always been in the state it was in now? When did something go from being real to less real and ultimately fake, given that the original was no longer around? Surely cereals today weren't anything like they had been in the past? Apples were nothing like the original apples because people had crossed different varieties. Dogs today were unlike the first dogs, which had been wolves, but surely that didn't make today's dogs any less real? Children born outside of marriage used to be stigmatised as illegitimate, but now they had been legitimised, along with test-tube babies and children conceived in a lab and hatched in wombs in India; it was a slippery slope. Some places were more real than others, according to Margrete, who would holiday in Hole in Hardangervidda National Park at Easter and in Kragerø on the coast in the summer, but what exactly did she mean? That the houses there had been preserved, that no new ones had been built or if they had, then built in the traditional style? Was authenticity linked to age, so that everything old was real, and yet not everything new could be branded as fake by that logic, could it? Surely a shopping centre could be just as real and authentic as an old church? The Hurtigruten ferry connecting Norway's coastal towns was real because the route itself was old, but the ships themselves were new; I was going around in circles. Can't you just churn out the stuff you usually do, I asked myself, like you used to do, to get the pitch finished because if old equals real and genuine, then surely the business pitches I produced before the postal directive were more real and authentic than what I was now writing in secret in the evenings, my writing style from the old days, from before Dag left, the second oldest in my repertoire. Come on, Ellinor, I told myself, just do it! You're not writing philosophy, just advertising copy! Follow the recipe! But I no longer wanted to do things by the book because all it generated was money, obviously, and people had to have it, I had to have it! I found myself simultaneously incapable of sticking to and straying from the beaten track because it's when you let go of it that things get complicated. At the same time you might find yourself in wonderfully unexpected places. When you ditch the script and the usual way of doing things, as Ibsen said: Where the starting point is maddest, the result is often the most original. But I wasn't striving for originality because that didn't exist – according to the film director Jim

Jarmusch – there was only authenticity, what did he mean by that? That there were no new existential questions, only new ways of discussing them and some people discussed them with greater impact than others and in their own unique way, with their own, unmistakable signature, something which I lacked. I suddenly realised that I had written: Am I real? No, I wrote. I exist in some way, I wrote, then I stopped. Perhaps I had to approach the concept of real via its opposite, fake? That which seeks to imitate. Like cheap goods made in China, bootleg copies of Western brands. Like I was trying to copy someone, but who? Like Dag, Rolf and me, that is all of Kraft-Kom, trying to copy Norway's leading PR agencies while simultaneously laying claim to originality and innovation. But the fake Gucci bags were actual bags even if they were made of plastic. They were real rip-offs! I realised that I was a genuine, pedigree imitator. So what, so what, I hammered away on my keyboard, we all mimic when we first learn to speak in order to communicate and I do want to communicate with other people, I typed, not just talk to myself, I wrote and collapsed over the laptop, exhausted.

Was the man behind the Real Thing himself the real thing, I wondered? I googled him; he looked like every other capitalist.

At night I sat in front of my laptop, working on a story about a PR consultant in crisis. He looked like Rolf, I called him Bjarne. Bjarne was struggling to come up with a good name for a fish restaurant in a neighbourhood with many other fish restaurants, all of which were vying to be the most real, the oldest and most authentic. There was The Genuine Old Fish Stall, and The Really Genuine Old Fish Stall, and The Genuinely Old Fish Stall with Genuinely Old and Real Fishermen Living in the Basement. Bjarne's initial proposal was The New Fish Restaurant Where the Genuinely Old Fishermen Have Moved In, but his boss, Børge, thought that was going too far, and Bjarne took offence and snapped that when he sat his exam at the School of Life, he got top marks.

Then I got stuck, I was being facetious and I deleted the file.

In the week between Christmas and New Year's Eve I started reading accounts of working conditions for postal workers in Germany and the Netherlands following the implementation of the EU's postal directive. They were impenetrable, to be frank. In order to extract their secrets I had to mobilise all my analytical skills. An hour later I had learned that postal workers no longer made enough to support themselves and that they lived in constant fear of what tomorrow would bring. Rolf and the head of Postkom had already explained this to me, but I wanted to find out for myself. Now that I'd had it confirmed, it should have outraged me, but I wasn't outraged at the persuasive conclusions drawn in the documents, merely irritated at the tediously repetitive and bureaucratic language. There were no cracks which the postal workers' fears and uncertain future could slip through. Their hardships and fears were documented in a verbose style and backed up with statistics that buried an immeasurable amount of mediocrity in cautious phrasing and circumspection. The term 'social dumping' was mentioned, but what it actually meant for the individual worker was lost in the obscure language, and I was reminded of Dag's note on the USB stick, about how decisions that would have a huge impact on people's lives were taken without asking or informing the people directly affected, in rooms with an absence of critical thinking.

I googled 'Helga Brun', but got no hits. Perhaps she never existed. Perhaps she was a metaphor. A reason for something, but what? I considered emailing Rudolph Karena Hansen to ask him to tell me the story, but decided instead to write him a letter which I folded and put in an envelope I'd had lying around since the days when we needed such things. I couldn't find a stamp so I drove to Oslo Central Station while reminiscing about the stamp albums of my childhood, the semi-profile of the British queen in different colours inserted in clear plastic pockets. Norway's post horn in different colours, the 25-øre stamp, the 10-øre stamp, and King Olav in semi-profile, also in different colours, how I had spent hours sorting and rating them, steaming letters over kettles, removing the stamps with a pair of tweezers and flapping them in the air to dry them while I dreamt about that rare stamp, the pearl in the oyster, the hidden treasure. Oslo Central Station was strangely deserted with just some of our new countrymen milling about in one corner while in another security guards were turfing out homeless people; the Narvesen kiosk was about to close. I asked what kind of stamps they sold and the woman looked at me blankly. She called out to a colleague who after much rummaging around found a stamp with a picture of Alexander Rybak costing 9.50 kroner and so I managed to post my letter at last. To say that the world was moving in favour of philatelists would be an exaggeration.

Ah, philatelists, I thought, they'll be on our side! Philatelists will support us, there are lots of them and most have the right to vote, the power to influence and a driving passion for stamps along with sentimentality, why has no one thought of them before? Philatelists of Norway unite against the EU's postal directive! Save the Post Office and Stamps for the People, I wrote once I got home, with the new king in profile, I added, because it was important to get the monarchists on board as well. Once again I was reminded of my childhood excitement at steaming stamps over the kettle and bashed the keyboard with renewed vigour. Long live the King and the royal family, I wrote, bursting with exuberance. Our quaint ambassadors for fjords and mountains and stamps. Our dogged and occasionally well-dressed champions, our timorous heartbeat's chosen ones, a source of comfort in times of hardship, leading actors in our anxious minds. We hail your blurred royalty! We celebrate our ageing Monarch, so lacking in pretension, and his cultured Queen with poems, paintings and presumably stamps, our unimpeachable Crown Prince so seemingly tender-hearted, our film star Crown Princess, our penitent Cinderella who gave a face to single mothers, the image of her naked body lives inside the heads of men of all ages in towns and villages, our whore and Madonna. We celebrate their duality and their duplicity, and our angelic Princess who talks to horses, dogs, daughters and the dead. In prison and in times of distress we want tiny squares of our better betters glued to our most important messages and tentative greetings and our Christmas cards because what would we do without them and their castle that stands full square like a stamp in the middle of a dangerous park guarded by men in horsehair helmets and holding shiny bayonets. Oh, royal family, royal ancestry of blue blood, older than the red post office, its high protectors, let yourselves be depicted so that you can be licked by our wet and willing tongues and thus ensure our missives reach their destination.

It was unusable. However, what mattered was my passion and commitment. Although it was ten thirty in the evening I called Rolf in a state of excitement. He didn't share my enthusiasm; the media training course was getting him down. I told him I'd had a flash of inspiration.

'Oh yes?'

I told him our mistake had been trying to describe a circle using only squares. He had no idea what I was talking about. I said that if you want to further your cause and that cause is change and making people care, then you can't subject it to a language which flattens mountains and puts out fires. He still had no idea what I meant.

'Would you', I asked him, 'trust a PR consultant to express your passion and your love, your deepest longing and its fulfilment, the energy and commitment needed to prevent the downfall of civilisation?'

'Have you been drinking?'

'I need to find better words,' I said. 'I need to find better images.'

'You do that,' he said and added 'Merry Christmas' before he hung up; I'd completely forgotten it was the holidays.

Describing a circle using circles, a triangle using triangles? It was easier said than done, how would I go about it? Stop describing what ought to be written and actually write it. The hardships and precarious future facing the German postal worker. The proud Norwegian postman's fear of losing hard-won workers' rights. I certainly couldn't do it, I was just another failed journalist. But perhaps life was like my experience in Ferner Jacobsen's menswear department, it wasn't about the words, but about the emotions that accompanied them. So I had to acquire them. And that, too, was easier said than done. Acquire emotion. Acquire is a strange word, but then again it was New Year's Eve. Stein was with his mother and his son, I had been invited to Margrete and Trond's, but preferred to be on my own. I had realised I had so much thinking to do, so much to experience. Our doubts exist only in our minds, but our despair fills every bit of us and can't be analysed; it must be lived through and I was impatient to get through it, who wouldn't want to get through the impossible as quickly as possible? I tried to recall how Dag smelled, I closed my eyes and tried to remember, I knew it was stored in my memory, suddenly it came back and Dag's smell filled me and filled the room and there was no escaping it. Not even in the hallway so I opened the front door to the stairwell to get some fresh air, but the stairwell, too, was dense with Dag's smell and I threw up and I screamed and cried and I lay down in an attempt to control the spasms.

I don't know how long I lay there; when I got up it was midnight and I felt empty as you do when you have expelled something that didn't agree with you. The King made his speech as usual, it was New Year's Eve and time for big words and big music and I stood in front of the living room window where I could see my own reflection and all the way to Nærsnes or possibly Slemmestad – the darkness made it impossible for me to get my bearings – but at the same time also easier as the woods and the sea disappeared while all the places where people lived were lit up. What's your purpose in life, I asked myself. Why exactly are you here? What's your role in society, what's your contribution?

Rolf's back was still playing up so I went to see the head of Postkom alone. I suggested writing an op-ed criticising the postal directive for one of the country's leading newspapers and getting all the General Council Members to sign it; I had read up on the TUC's structure after Christmas and knew what a General Council Member was. I also suggested starting a petition against the postal directive, not unlike the one Dag had started in the run-up to the 2009 general election; I had ploughed through the head of Postkom's email correspondence with Dag between Christmas and the New Year. One hundred and fifty-one mayors had signed to say that they feared the quality and service of the Post Office would plummet if the directive was implemented, and that they expected the government as a minimum to ask for a derogation like eleven EU countries had already done. It hadn't been given the attention it deserved at the time, but it was good to know that so many important people were on my, or rather, our side. The mayor of Arendal and the mayors of Askvold and Audnedal, of Åfjord, Ål, Åmot and Ås. In the office next to mine, but without me knowing it, Dag had emailed every single mayor in the country, and although not all of them had replied, one hundred and fifty-one mayors representing every single political party had. I guessed that Dag had called, argued, pushed, convinced, lobbied while I had been slumped over another mind-numbing issue of ByggBo or researching how to market restaurant chains. Now I wanted to start a similar petition, based on Dag's work, Dag's words and upload it to www.postdirektivet.no. The head of Postkom thought it was a great idea, and I went to the office determined to write so that not only those already converted but people in general, shop assistants in menswear departments and skiers and bankers, would understand that the directive was a terrible idea and that's when I realised I'd never asked Stein what had happened to that bank job he had applied for, and that I hadn't bought a present for Truls, yet again I had forgotten all about him.

After work I popped into Steen & Strøm's toy department. When I was almost there I felt like turning back, then I went in anyway. I couldn't remember the last time I had visited a toy shop, I tried to remember one of my old toys, I must have had some? A shadow fell across me, I looked around to see what had caused it, but there were no windows, the shelves were stuffed with toys in every colour right up to the ceiling and there were toys hanging from the ceiling, but there were no windows, I rushed outside. In the street I got my breath back and I went to a bookshop instead. It was airy and had windows, I bought a Postman Pat book. Stein said I was welcome to come over now although Truls wasn't there.

I decided to walk up the stairs, it eased my breathlessness. Stein was in the doorway on his crutches and we hugged, his mother had gone out shopping, it was fine, I wouldn't be staying long. He asked if I wanted coffee, I didn't, I put the present for Truls on the table and was going to ask him about the bank, then I thought maybe he hadn't got the job and my asking might upset him. He asked if I wanted tea, I said yes, and once we had sat down with it, I told him that I'd started crying during the media training course last month and so the course had to finish early.

'Really?' he said, 'why,' he asked, he was surprised, practically lost for words.

'I've even started thinking I should change jobs,' I blurted out, 'but I've no idea what I would do instead. Everyone has to earn a living.'

'That's just it,' he said and chewed his lip, and his mother came back and I walked down the stairs wondering whether it was the end or the beginning.

Rolf was still unwell so I took over the postal directive. Every time the head of Postkom had a meeting, he would call and update me. He was visiting several of Labour's county branches prior to their annual conferences to fan the flames of opposition. If they subsequently voted against the directive, he would visit them again or call to find out which arguments had won the day. He would then pass that information on to me. Thus he spent his days travelling and on the phone, and from his iPhone he commented on my ideas for the petition and one cold January day it was ready. I posted the petition on www.postdirektivet.no and less than an hour later the signatures started pouring in. I checked several times a day and every time there were new names, on some days several hundred, the bush telegraph, I thought, it's spreading like wildfire, there's a good reason for these clichés, from now on I wouldn't ridicule them unless they were being used as empty phrases, not if they were meant sincerely. To say what you mean, that's what it's all about! The first thing I did when I got up in the morning was to visit www.postdirektivet.no and check and every day there would be more, and the January darkness was no longer quite so dark and the cold loosened its grip and the queue of traffic on Mosseveien wasn't as slow as usual, and who knew perhaps opponents of the postal directive were inside those cars.

By the end of January seven Labour county conferences had voted against it. Many of their delegates would be attending the party's annual conference mandated by their branch. No county conference had voted in favour, and the few county conferences where the majority against had been small had all had visits from members of the government. However, in Møre and Romsdal where the foreign minister, Jonas Gahr Støre, had urged members to vote No to the resolution opposing the directive, all but four people voted in favour of it once Støre had left and the issue was put to the vote. Surely that suggested the party leadership knew something was up? Did they have a plan and could the head of Postkom get a clue as to what it was? He investigated using his considerable network and I tried to put myself in the shoes of the prime minister and the Cabinet, but it was difficult. Labour in government was the enemy, that much I knew. I knew my enemy, but he wasn't visible on the battlefield. Senior Labour politicians were forever in the news defending the bombing of Libya, but they never once mentioned the postal directive. Those in favour of the directive were notably absent. The head of Postkom sat in his office in Møllergata 10 and tried to work out why that was, I listened and learned. Did they have something up their sleeve, he wondered. Would there be a sudden change, an ambush when we least expected it? He said 'we'.

No, he reasoned. But the government knew it was an unpopular issue which it was best not to bring up. Let sleeping dogs lie. They expected to get their way as usual.

'But they underestimate us,' the head of Postkom said, he was counting on me and rubbed his hands eager to fight. I sincerely hoped he was right. I really did. Shortly after I had left and was crossing Møllergata, he opened a window and called out to me: 'Sunndal city council has voted against it!'

Political decisions impact on people's lives, I knew that, that was the point. What's agreed in Parliament will have consequences for the population, me included. I didn't smoke in places where smoking wasn't permitted – on the odd occasion I smoked. Extended opening hours for shops had made life simpler for many, for me, but I had never thought about the impact on shop assistants, I hadn't understood all the unintended consequences. If the EU's third postal directive was passed, postal workers risked having their wages cut, not in theory, but for real. Not being able to pay your mortgage. Having to sell your car. Applying for benefits in order to get by. It could happen to anyone. No, it couldn't, that was the problem! People like me would always be able to get a well-paid job, I could always ask my mum for help, there was no risk for me or the prime minister or the foreign minister, what did it mean for society that the most privileged were always out of the danger zone? Were they even capable of understanding the worries of the postal worker? Was I capable of understanding the worries of the postal worker?

Probably not, but at least I was trying to put myself in their shoes. I tried to imagine what it was like to be the prime minister in order to understand what he thought about the postal directive. I tried to imagine what it was like to be the consumer in order to understand how I could trick her into thinking she needed, say, the Real Thing. I could try to imagine what it might be like to be anyone. But how could I really know what that was like when I had huge problems understanding myself, when I didn't even know myself properly, when I wasn't even on first-name terms with myself, so to speak? But what if, it occurred to me, the path to knowing myself went through others? I could try to empathise with other people for no other reason than because we shared the human condition. Because others might share my struggle and they might be able to help me. I needed help and I needed it now, I didn't want to put my life on hold like Margrete, I didn't want to defer life until it was more convenient because tomorrow might not come and it could all be over. I had a hunch that life had taught other people lessons and that it would do me good to talk to them.

One afternoon there was a letter from Rudolf Karena Hansen in my letter box. I ran upstairs with it and sat down in fear and trembling. He wrote that he was working on a big book on Helga Brun and for that reason he couldn't give too much away because he had heard that PR consultants were thieving magpies.

~

129

After thinking it over, I wrote back humbly to say I was hard at work on the postal directive and that I had a feeling the story of Helga Brun could help inspire opposition to it and contribute to a victory, I was no longer so daunted by big words. He wrote back saying I was welcome to visit him in Eiby.

Two weeks later I got on a plane. We took off when it was dark and landed in even deeper darkness, I feared the darkness. In Oslo the days had started getting longer, but it wasn't clear to me what was actually light and what was in my mind. Perhaps I was psychotic or in the manic phase of a bipolar episode and now the darkness was coming back. The piles of snow were high as mountains, it was like driving through the bottom of a canyon, the taxi driver knew Rudolf Karena Hansen well. He pointed out the old church and the former sawmill, the former school, the closed-down café and pulled up at a not-yet-former farm where light shone through the ground-floor windows and told me to say hi from Kai.

I waited outside while I plucked up the courage to ring the bell. Rudolf Karena Hansen soon appeared on the doorstep wearing a knitted jumper similar to the one I had returned to the skier, and I was invited into his smell, pipe tobacco, log fire and beard. We said hello and I passed on Kai's greeting, oh that Kai, Rudolf Karena Hansen said, and led me into a living room filled with greying books about Finnmark during the war and the scorched-earth tactic and Chinese postmen.

He gave me a drink, one for the road he called it though I hadn't been doing any driving. I didn't want to drink it. Nor did I want to put it down, I drank it and felt warm, I was offered a chair and a waffle biscuit he had baked himself because his wife was ill in bed upstairs and would bang a stick on the floor whenever she needed him. Right, he said, tilting his head towards the ceiling, I heard soft thuds, then he left and didn't come back for quite some time. Nordahl Grieg's poem 'Morning over Finnmark' written in an old-fashioned, joined-up hand was pinned to the wall with a drawing pin. I read about when they reached Mount Bæskades and a storm was brewing and they stopped because the reindeers were tired. One of them stamped its hoof, 'and cut deep into the frozen earth, where lumps of blue-green lichen burst forth like light against its muzzle'. His 'rootless heart', Grieg wrote, had chased him far across the mountains, filled with dreams of love and a zest for life. Now he wondered if he had ever stood like the reindeer. Never! And yet he had enjoyed the gifts of the land, which those before him had built and toiled for. What was his contribution?

What was mine?

The question made me uncomfortable, but surely it wasn't too late to start? I certainly hadn't run across the country filled with dreams of love and a zest for life.

When Rudolf came back, he refilled our glasses, drained his own and poured himself another before his face adopted a solemn expression.

~

His book about Helga Brun would be a great and important philosophical work, the like of which the world had never seen. But it took time to write a tome like that, of course, and to be an author when you were also a husband and a postman responsible for making dead letters live again, well, it seemed like a kind of infidelity.

I said I understood.

As a result he had got no further than the preface, he said, he was, however, terrifically pleased with it. Because what you write at the start of a preface, he said, will be different from what you write at the end, writing a preface was like fighting your way through an impenetrable jungle with no paths and suddenly coming out the other side and not knowing where you are, but it's still wonderful to have got through it!

I had no idea what he meant, but emerging from the wilderness must be nice.

'Whoever writes about Helga Brun', he said, 'will have to forge their own path and not be afraid of the authorities and not do the bidding of the establishment, or be for sale, they must be someone the powerful will need to watch out for!'

There was thumping from upstairs and he left the room. Once he came back, he poured himself another drink, emptied his glass and refilled it, then asked me about the postal directive.

'Expensive, bad, Oslo-centric,' I said, quoting www. postdirektivet.no.

'Exactly, exactly,' he said, 'we can't say that often enough!'

I told him about the head of Postkom's indefatigable efforts on the phone and on the road, about the encouraging No votes at the Labour Party's county conferences and the petition which 6,333 people had signed so far, and which would he please promote on his route? Because if the 3,303 inhabitants he delivered post to all signed it, it would make a difference, perhaps they had already become 3,313?

'3,308 as of today,' he said and told me about dramatic births when the hospital was far away and the roads were closed due to storms across Mount Bæskades.

A pause ensued and I plucked up the courage.

'So, Helga Brun?' I prompted him.

'Yes, Helga,' he said, adopting a solemn expression once more, it is right to talk about expression in this instance. He scrutinised me and I blushed, thereby disqualifying myself from hearing the story of Helga, I imagined.

'Ultimately it's a shocking and yet enjoyable story,' he said, 'definitely a dreadful one.'

'I would like to hear it,' I said, 'because I suspect I might learn something from it,' I said, 'which might prove useful in the resistance fight.'

He nodded pensively.

June 1967 on Sørøy. Helga is wearing a yellow dress and arrives on the steamer to teach at the summer school held every year so the island's children will have something to do while their parents work full-time at the fish market and at the fish factory. Just under 1,500 people live on the island, it's exciting whenever a new person arrives, no matter how long they stay. Helga is welcomed by the island's two resident teachers who have yet to start their holidays. They help her get settled in Mrs Rasmussen's attic flat where the summer-school teachers usually stay. Helga is twenty-six years old and not particularly attractive. She has blonde hair, a calm, blue gaze and a mild, soft voice, she is like summer-school teachers on Sørøy tend to be and have been for years. She is shown around the island and introduced to the island's other figures of authority, the doctor, the vicar and the sheriff. They meet other inhabitants on their way from the school to the shop and the post office, the church, the harbour and the petrol station. Helga doesn't cause much of a stir except possibly among the young men from the village, most are fishermen working tough shifts and in their spare time they hang around the small harbour café. Early summer was a good time on Sørøy, the days were growing longer, the temperature was rising and the tourists had started coming, but not too many of them yet. The shrill whistle of the steamer and the hoarse screeching of the seagulls, both reassuring sounds that everything is as it should be, amid repetition and the rhythms of nature, the whispering of the waves and the chirping of the birds, he was setting the scene just like we had done during the media training course.

Helga came, saw and smiled an enigmatic smile and in the late evenings would sit on the long swing that hung from the big aspen tree on the common in the endless, sun-filled and yet almost white evenings before the sky would suddenly explode in red like a blazing fire. Helga swung on the swing and went for long walks on the island's paths across the mountains and along the jetties and to the beaches without jetties and anyone who was awake could watch her throw stone after stone into the sea, as if she was unburdening herself of something. But that's easy to say with hindsight because hindsight is afterwards and not before, like the difference between the first and the last sentence in a preface.

One teacher spent the first week with her, on the first day of the second week she was on her own and taught the children aged seven to thirteen about photosynthesis and the capitals of Europe before taking them on a field trip and teaching them the names of the birds in the air and the flowers in the fields that didn't regret yesterday or dread tomorrow, but lived only for today. A few people think, Helga added, that being happy in the present moment is easier said than done, but there is some dispute about that. Many people watched from their kitchen windows, smiling at the sight of this cheerful group, the island's future, playing and learning out in God's green earth, and thought it looked like a scene from *The Sound of Music* with the majestic snow-capped mountains in the background. As everyone knows the film has a happy ending, and they, too, would enjoy a happy ending this year, they thought, as they had the year before and the year before that. During the last lesson on the Friday of the first week, Helga gave the children of Sørøy an essay assignment and they walked home in silence. The next day they sat in their rooms, each on their own, working on the essay without putting a single word on paper. The mothers who sneaked into their children's rooms at night after they had fallen asleep discovered when they peeked at the worksheets that the children had been hunched deep in concentration but without writing a single word. The children's serious faces in the morning, the children's brooding, the children's long, solitary bike rides, something had changed them and it had to be that essay. The parents asked the children about their homework, but no one said anything. The parents told them not to worry about the essay and the summer school, it was only pretend school with no exam so, strictly speaking, there was no need to hand in the essay. But it had no effect. The children sat over their worksheets lost in something the grown-ups didn't know and couldn't make them snap out of.

But then a father met a mother in the street, then a mother met a mother down at the quay, and another mother and father met in the shop, and although it was deeply personal and associated with feelings of shame and vulnerability, although it felt like revealing a weakness, they started to ask cautiously: 'That essay the children are working on . . .'

'Oh yes, that.'

'They don't seem to be finding it very easy.'

'No, you can say that again.'

'And we can't get them to stop worrying about it either.'

'You're right there too.'

'And it's supposed to be about . . .'

'Yes, now what was it, it's completely slipped my mind.'

'Mine too.'

'But Pål might remember.'

'Yes, Pål, who is just over there, he's bound to know.'

But Pål didn't know and the tension rose on Sørøy and people thought enough was enough and decided to find out what was going on, but when they came home, the children were bent eagerly over their worksheets, writing so the ink spluttered and they didn't disturb their parents while they watched the last episode of *The Forsyte Saga* on the television, and once the children had started writing, the problem solved itself because the parents could simply check the worksheets once the children were asleep. However, when the children had finished writing they didn't go to bed, they ran out into the Sunday evening as if it was a matter of urgency, as if they couldn't get rid of their essays fast enough, to post their densely filled worksheets through Helga Brun's letter box that sat innocently next to that of Mrs Rasmussen on a stand by the entrance to the house, but then they grew anxious that someone might steal or sneak a peek at them and so they rang the bell on Mrs Rasmussen's door to ask if the summer-school teacher, Helga Brun, was in. And of course she was. This happened sixteen times Helga Brun came down that evening to receive essays from her pupils and stayed up until late into the night to read them. From the kitchen windows and the living room windows the parents glanced nervously at Helga's window where the light was on even during the short night.

Monday morning no one on Sørøy was able to wake their children. The parents shook them and shouted at them, but soon had to go to work at the highly regarded firm of undertakers or the not-quite-so-highly-regarded shop or the fish market or the harbour café, and left the children to the old folks who didn't care because it was pretend school with no exams. Helga sat alone in the classroom with her knitting and her face calm, said those who walked past in the street and looked in. The children were still asleep when their parents came home from work, but late that afternoon they woke up and wandered about as if in a daze, their eyes eerily dark, it was impossible to meet them without shuddering and their voices had deepened during the last twenty-four hours and nothing was as it normally was on Sørøy in the middle of June, and someone must be to blame. But how to lance the boil and who would throw the first stone? The vicar went to see the doctor and the doctor and the vicar went to see the owner of the petrol station and the manager of the café and the landlady and the fish market manager and a few claim that the postmaster was there too, but there's some doubt about that. After speaking to everyone, the adults agreed to turn up at the school on Tuesday morning before the children arrived and demand an explanation from Helga Brun. But when they woke up Tuesday morning, the children were already out of their beds and had run to school without any breakfast, so impatient were they to hear what Helga Brun had to say about their essays.

They sat on tenterhooks when Helga entered with the essays under her arm. Fortunately she had had twenty-four hours to reflect on them, she sat down and was about to open her mouth when the adults, led by the vicar and the doctor, marched into the room and demanded to know the title of the essay.

'Why am I unhappy,' Helga said in her calm manner.

There was silence for six seconds, then the adults surged forwards, their hands reaching for the pile; the children realised what was happening and what it entailed so they, too, ran forwards with their hands outstretched, screaming and protesting, and the adults swore and kicked and lashed out, and the smallest children wriggled in between the adults to get to the essays, a jumble of everyone against everyone, driven by the same urgency, dozens of small hands and big hands grabbing at the delicate papers which were torn to shreds between fearful, frantic fingers, the children stuffed the scraps into their mouths and swallowed them, in less than a minute the pile was pulverised from the shared desire of everyone involved, a desire for annihilation.

Only Helga Brun had read them. The adults decided on the spot that she was fired and would be sent back on the first boat. A few whispered suggestions for more drastic measures, but the most respected among them didn't want to court unnecessary controversy. Trust us, they whispered. A young, blonde girl in a yellow dress taking action against us? There's no danger of that, they whispered, and the essays no longer exist, it'll be one person's word against many others, claims without evidence which no one will believe. But the children? The children are just that, children, you tell them bedtime stories at night which they've forgotten the next morning, they'll grow out of it. So they marched Helga down to the quay and paid for her steamer ticket all the way to Alta where she was from and where she could probably manage. They never heard from Helga again, as far as they were concerned she might as well be dead, and ultimately they would have preferred that. Life went back to normal, and when the anxious summer and the subsequent dark winter was over, everyone had stopped worrying, and it was summer once more because nature repeats herself, but fortunately without incident this time because no Helga appeared, instead a harmless, fifty-year-old Ågot who on her first day of teaching at the summer school gave the children on Sørøy an essay with the title: 'The biggest fish my father ever caught'. Everyone breathed a sigh of relief, the danger had passed.

We sat in silence for a long time.

After possibly five minutes – my sense of time was not what it usually was – there was thumping from the first floor, and

Rudolf Karena Hanson slowly rose to his feet. 'You can imagine the rest yourself,' he said.

But I couldn't imagine the rest, I had to be spoon fed. When he came back, he asked where I would be staying the night as if he was worried that I was expecting to stay with him, but I had booked a hotel. He had had enough of me, he had other things to do, his sick wife upstairs and a pile of dead letters.

'But,' I said, 'the letters to Helga Brun written all those years later, they weren't sent from Sørøy, but from Drammen, weren't they?'

'Yes, they were,' he said and closed his mouth.

I couldn't leave now. Leaving now was impossible. He asked me about the postal directive again, but I didn't want to talk about the postal directive, it was trivial and political and so far away from what I felt I was close to, I was approaching something major and I didn't want to return to minor, he fixed his gaze on me.

'It's serious,' he said.

'Yes,' I said, because it was.

'It's either or, life or death,' he said.

'Yes,' I said.

'With every breath, every step, every decision,' he said.

'Yes,' I said, but it didn't feel like it, it felt impossible.

'It's not impossible', he said as if he could read my mind, 'to be equally serious in minor as well as major things, in the detail as well as in the bigger picture.'

There was thumping from upstairs and he got up.

'If, as a child, you were told that breaking your leg was a sin, you would be scared of breaking it and probably break it more often, don't you think?'

'Yes?'

He left the room and went upstairs, I didn't understand what he was saying, I wasn't afraid of breaking my leg even though Stein had broken his foot, so what was I afraid of? When he came back, he had a piece of paper in his hand.

'If you want an easy life,' he said, 'all you have to do is make yourself insignificant. Believe in one thing today, another tomorrow and something completely different by the end of the week, turn yourself into several people and parcel yourself out, have one anonymous opinion and another in your own name, one spoken, one written, one on the Internet, another in the shop and a third as a lover, yet another as a PR consultant, or as a private individual and another with Postkom, and then all your troubles will go away, you'll see.'

I closed my eyes, but to no avail, I started to cry. He put his hand on my shoulder, I let out a few sobs, then it eased off. He gave me the piece of paper in his hand, a copy of the letter to Helga Brun. He had been given permission to make it, he assured me, by Helga herself on her deathbed; once she had read it, she could die in peace. The letter was written by a female pupil from Helga's week on Sørøy.

Dear Helga Brun,

It has been more than forty years, but I can't forget what happened and I'm writing to you now to thank you for the essay assignment. I had felt so alone, so ashamed of myself, only I didn't realise it. When I wrote the essay, something unravelled inside me and the process began. I found the courage to accept myself, my unhappiness, my imperfections and my strength, and I was able to take responsibility for myself. I was reconciled with the human condition on this earth, I was able to see that life is a gift and to treasure it. That's the challenge and we should be grateful for it and take it seriously. It was in the summer of '67 that I took the first step up from the basement. Many people live in the basement even though there is room at the top where the view is wider and the outlook broader and where fear of the future and the unknown can be turned into anticipation.

Yours devotedly, EJ
Drammen

I took the copy of the letter, thanked him, bowed and promised to stand my ground. The taxi arrived with Kai behind the wheel, in my hotel room I read the letter again. Self-acceptance, was that what I was struggling with, was that what I was longing for? To accept myself as I truly was, my childhood, my story, my mum, my sister, my job history, my shortcomings and my apathy, the whole package. And that was just for starters. And then take responsibility for myself and my actions and my growth. Not blame them on external circumstances, though these obviously played a part. Not blame society, though it obviously provided the framework for my activities and my being, I had choices, the choices were queuing up from when I got up in the morning till I went to bed at night, I had a choice right now whether or not to call Stein and tell him about Helga Brun.

I stood by the window in my hotel room and convinced myself that behind the storm, which was brewing outside, I could make out Mount Bæskades, while I reassessed my own story which I hadn't understood was unbearable until Dag died. At that point I had already discovered my old diary from 2000 and was teetering on the edge, then Dag died and nudged me, I fell and I hurt myself, but I got up again and now I was here. A mere mortal, but perhaps that was enough? Might life be a serious business that required something of you, a daunting enterprise? The thought, however, wasn't oppressive but liberating because it's good to have a purpose, to be given a purpose, it's a declaration of trust because you don't entrust a task to someone you don't respect. It was almost as if I, too, was standing on the bottom step of a dark basement staircase and could see dawn creep under the door at the top, and I was filled with great faith that I would make it all the way up and step out into the bright ground floor.

I wanted to call Stein and share everything with him, but I didn't, you don't become spontaneous overnight. I imagined Stein as he walked down Rosenkrantz' gate on the way to the restaurant to meet his girlfriend, stiff and straining, and felt a new tenderness for him, why hadn't I noticed before that he, too, was teetering on the edge.

I called him from the airport the next day: 'Guess where I am?'

'Where are you?'

'Alta!'

'Alta? What are you doing up there?'

'I had a meeting with a postman.'

'Go on?'

As he said nothing more I realised that he could tell this was no ordinary phone call or ordinary postman.

'It's for work,' I said.

'Aha?'

'You know I'm working on the postal directive.'

'I thought you were working on the Real Thing?'

'Yes, that too, for as long as it lasts. I want to tell you about the postal directive once I get home.'

'When will that be?'

'Soon. How are things?'

'All right.'

'I just wanted to let you know where I was.'

He was silent for a few seconds, there was a noise I could barely hear, then he said: 'I'm glad you called.'

When I turned on my phone again at Gardermoen airport, I received a text message from the head of Postkom. The Trom branch of the Christian People's Party had passed a resolution

145

opposing the directive. It wasn't much but . . . When could I deliver the op-ed?

I hadn't done much work on it yet so I called Rolf and asked if I could drop by.

He was in bed nursing his bad back. In a professional but at the same time sincere tone of voice, I hoped, I told him that although the media course hadn't gone according to plan, the head of Postkom was delighted. Several county conferences, local government leaders, the senior leadership of Young Friends of the Earth as well as the Trom branch of the Christian People's Party had all passed resolutions opposing the directive.

'The Christian People's Party?' he groaned, clasping his back.

'There's now a chance of reaching a compromise with the Labour leadership.'

He rocked back and forth as people with a bad back tend to do.

'I found a memory stick in Dag's office.'

'Aha?'

'There was nothing personal on it.'

'Why would there be?'

'So I thought that we for his sake—?'

'Forget it!'

'He writes explicitly that if the postal directive is passed then you can't be sure that your letter will be delivered.'

'My letter?'

'Perhaps that explains why you haven't had a letter from Dag. It got lost in the EU because of the postal directive.'

'Seriously, Ellinor.'

'Why is that so hard to imagine? Anyway, I've been wondering if you could join the Labour Party.'

'I beg your pardon?'

'One of us needs to attend their annual conference.'

'Are you out of your mind?'

'It doesn't have to be a lost cause! I've been working really hard on the postal directive while you've been off sick. I know you voted Labour last year.'

'I did not.'

'You said you did.'

'I can't remember what I voted last year. You join.'

'That's impossible.'

'Why?'

'It just is.'

'And why would it be impossible for you, but possible for me.'

'Because I'm on a journey towards . . . the truth.'

I regretted saying it immediately.

'Eh?'

'Oh, forget it. You'll be paid double.'

'What?'

'You heard me. Join the Labour Party and get paid double, you're the one who knows all the lobby correspondents.'

I bent down and looked him in the eye.

'I need you,' I said, he turned his face to the side, he was embarrassed. That evening he texted me to say we had a deal.

~

I was delighted and called Stein to tell him I was back.

'Yes,' he said in a quizzical voice, but there was nothing more I wanted to say or was there?

'I had a strange experience in Alta,' I said.

'Yes?'

But where should I begin?

'Yes?' he said again, and then I remembered that he was on the edge and if I didn't get it right, I might get it badly wrong, and I said that the right words were proving hard to find and that I couldn't articulate what I wanted to say. He said he knew what I meant because he often felt that way, then he said that he was going on a winter holiday with his mother and Truls. He paused and then he said that he had missed me.

Again the words eluded me, but at least he knew what that was like, we said goodbye, I didn't regret having called him.

Spring had to be the reason. March and the light in March and a few coltsfoot shoots on the verges. Tender new trees that looked as if their keen, green leaves made them bashful, the older trees stood guard, the birds flew between them with twigs in their beaks, building nests for which they needed no planning permission. Rolf had read the two files on Dag's memory stick and grown pensive. We were pensive at the office and opened the windows when the sun was high in the sky and heard the birds chirping and free. We've put on our thinking caps, we would say when we bumped into each other in the corridor or in the kitchen after having sat for a long time at our respective desks hunched over foreign newspapers and magazines trying to understand the EU, EFTA and neoliberalism. It's not all bad to have to put my thinking cap on again, Rolf said, and I knew what he meant, we were on the right track. We learned and understood and tried to think new thoughts, it was a blessed relief and although we became increasingly conscious of our impotence, at least we were no longer lying to ourselves. We were horrified that the left was working to accept and adapt to existing conditions rather than trying to change them, that the left opted to support the superficial rather than the fundamental, parental leave and the Sex Purchase Act rather than campaign for a new financial world order that would rein in the predatory and the greedy. It was good to share the work, and to work in Dag's spirit as it was before he gave up and quit. We sat in the kitchen with coffee and remembered him as he had been towards the end, even more hunched, a sombre, conflicted figure we saw too late, a dark cloud dissolving. Dag at sea in his boat, drawing up his life's balance sheet. When did it start to go wrong, when did the downward spiral begin? When he gave up politics for journalism? When he gave up journalism in the hope of making money as a PR consultant? When it became clear that he wouldn't get rich from his PR firm, when he gave up becoming rich in other ways, when it was suddenly too late? When his wife left him and he lost faith in the postal directive?

'Spring is definitely here,' Rolf said and spent the ever-lighter evenings with his neighbour, the Labour veteran Thor

Granengren, who knew the party's organisation, the TUC, other Labour veterans and key people all over the country. I was alone with my thinking cap on while Rolf took over the daily conversations with the head of Postkom and was on the phone from morning to night with people from near and far. I worked on the op-ed which was scheduled to be published the day before Labour's annual conference and hopefully signed by several trade union leaders, and it was becoming a matter of urgency. I had started it many times, but was unable to write something you can read while having your afternoon nap. I threw in the towel on Wednesday, handed over the job to Rolf and drove to Bygdøy to clear my head because blue anemones grew in the forest on Bygdøy and they calmed me down. While I was on Bygdøy between the blue sea and the blue flowers, Margrete called to tell me she was pregnant. She didn't wait for me to react, she just carried on talking and said that they had decided not to tell anyone until after the first three months, but that she couldn't help herself. I had to promise not to tell Stein and not let Trond know that she had told me, and not a word to Mum, it could go wrong again, but this time it was three weeks longer than last time and after all, I was the person closest to her.

That got me thinking. Even though she had said I was the person closest to her in the same way she had said that all good things come in threes at Christmas, and said it because it's what you say to your sister, it still got me thinking. But was she serious? I didn't think so. But if she truly felt I was the closest she had, did that make me so? And if it did, what did that entail?

'Imagine, you're going to be an auntie,' she said, 'unless something goes wrong, of course.'

'I'm sure it'll be fine,' I said.

'I'm so happy,' she said, 'and so scared,' she said, 'it's so strange, everything is mixed up in a huge feeling with no name.'

She invited us to Sunday lunch. You both, she said, she must mean Stein and me, I thanked her and congratulated her once more, but then realised I hadn't congratulated her the first time. Thank you, she said, and we rang off and I was going to ring Stein. But first I wanted to let the news sink in. I leaned against a tree and closed my eyes and imagined Margrete with a baby. It was a lovely image. Margrete smiling at the child as I had never seen her smile before. The background was more troubling. Auntie Ellinor standing stiffly next to the mother. I wouldn't be able to pull it off. I had the script in my hand, but I was incapable of playing my part.

I hadn't been to Stein's flat since I came back from Finnmark. I was scared of nudging him and scared of telling him about Helga Brun and the postal directive in case it would be a damp squib, I didn't want it to be an anti-climax! But now I called him to ask if he wanted to come for Sunday lunch at Margrete's, and he asked where I was, perhaps he could hear the seagulls and the rustling of the trees. When I said Bygdøy, he said he could be there shortly, he was driving back from seeing a physiotherapist who had told him that walking on uneven surfaces would do him good.

We met in the car park a little later and he took my arm, it was strange, but also possible that he did so because of his broken foot. I hadn't rehearsed what to say, perhaps that explained why I was nervous and asked him about the bank, if he liked his job. He didn't reply 'yes' as I had expected, and even as I asked him the question I knew it was a stupid thing to ask, a small-talk question to which he would say yes, and we would both be none the wiser. He said: 'That depends on what you mean by like.'

If he was serious, then it was a big question. When I didn't reply immediately, he squeezed my arm, perhaps it was all in my mind, but it was just the nudge I needed. I said I had been wondering if it was a job he would like to do for many years. I said I had been wondering if he found it meaningful. And I didn't stop there, I asked if it was his dream job. But it couldn't possibly be, so I added: What would be your ideal job, what do you dream about?

We reached the tree I had been leaning against before without him saying anything. I wondered if I should ask if he was free for Sunday lunch to help him along, but when I glanced at him sideways, I saw that his eyebrows were knitted as if in pain and a shiver went through me. I bent down to the ground, picked up a stone and threw it in the water. 'Well, here's the thing,' he said in a strange and soft voice, 'I don't dream about anything.'

We walked back to the car park in silence, he had parked next to mine because we knew each other's cars. We knew quite a lot. He accepted the invitation to Sunday lunch, I said I would write him a letter.

'A letter?'

'Yes. A good old-fashioned letter.'

There was something I had to tell him, but which I couldn't tell him.

'Dear Stein,'

I wrote with a new pen on a new white sheet of paper and dated it in the top right-hand corner, 21 March, Labour's annual conference was eighteen days away. Then I rested the pen against the paper, leaving a big blue stain, but it didn't matter.

'I feel as if my life is too banal for my despair. That our relationship is too trivial and not passionate enough for our despair. What do we do with our despair if our lives are too small to contain it? Deny our despair and ignore our beating hearts, remain at odds with ourselves and fight ourselves, or accept that there's so much we'll never understand intellectually and try to live with things which don't add up, that what's most important might be something we can only just sense, and teach our brains to illuminate our hearts and help us live with contradictions that can't be cancelled out and become open to the idea that being a mere mortal is enough, more than enough in most respects, and once we're alive, try to live with gratitude and passion rather than shame and paralysis.'

I stopped, I felt the kind of relief you experience after you have thrown up.

I couldn't send it of course. Not that it mattered. But I had to write something because I had promised him a letter, and a letter is practically a gift. I drove to the stationers to buy a pale green sheet of paper because green is a hopeful colour and a slightly darker pine green envelope, just for the fun of it, and went home and stared at the paper for a long time. I got up without having written anything and walked in circles on the floor, then I sat down again and stayed there for a long time. Finally I wrote 'I love you', it came from deep inside me, and perhaps it wasn't true. I folded the sheet of paper neatly, put it in the envelope and wrote his name on it while I imagined him on Rosenkrantz' gate and relived our meeting on Bygdøy and stuck on a stamp with a picture of a sculpture by Arnold Haukeland, which I had bought during one of my now quite frequent visits to post offices in recent months. I also sprayed a little perfume on it.

The next morning when I got up and saw the letter lying on the chest of drawers in the hall ready for its enigmatic journey, I visualised the words inside it and felt that they were truer now than before I wrote them, that words once written become true. I stopped at the Narvesen kiosk in Holtet and dropped it into the post box. He would get it as early as tomorrow if what it said on the post box was true, and I believed it. I had great faith in the Post Office, in all of this invisible machinery which would ensure that the letter I had dropped into the red post box today at a quarter to four would be in Stein's green letter box sometime between ten and two o'clock tomorrow, depending on the route of the local postman.

On Wednesday, the week after I gave him the job, Rolf delivered a perfectly acceptable draft of the op-ed. I commented on it and improved it, simply and joyfully, and it was a relief that it wasn't either or, but both and. We need to act in this world and write something you can read while taking your afternoon nap. But never lose sight of the words of the unknown EJ from Drammen. Someone had to use the big words, I whispered to myself. They had gone out of fashion, I realised as I came across them unexpectedly and started listening to people's vocabulary in a new way, taking their language literally and searching for the message in it. There were plenty of fine words being bandied around, there was inflation in fine phrases, but the big words were noticeable by their absence. Still they had been invented by mere mortals once, and in the evenings I would stand in front of the mirror and say them out loud and eventually without any inhibitions: Endless, insight, resolution, reconciliation, freedom, clarity, fraternity, and many more.

Eight thousand people had signed the online petition, and yet no one knew about it. The postal directive seemed to be a secret. It didn't feel like that when we visited Møllergata 10, but the moment we stepped outside among people rushing about and shopping and sitting on café chairs wearing sunglasses, the postal directive became unreal. People couldn't relate to the postal directive. Trying to hold onto the importance of the postal directive was a challenge when the world was uninformed, uninterested. Occasionally we would bump into someone we knew when we crossed Egertorget on the way to our own offices and would stop for a chat. When they asked where we had been, we would blush. We're working on opposing the introduction of the EU's postal directive, one of us would say at times whereupon they would change the subject immediately.

It was 24 March and two weeks to Labour's annual conference. Eleven thousand people had signed the petition. The TUC leadership had agreed a resolution against the directive, it was my job to make these facts known. I wrote press releases and sent them out, but no one published them in full. A few local newspapers printed short notices on the second to last page in between advertising. *Romerikes Blad* was supportive, but that was mostly for old times' sake, would be my guess. Radio and television didn't care. Every time an unknown number called, I hoped that it would be a journalist wanting to know what was happening with the postal directive, but it never was. Journalists, where are you, I felt like shouting, but they were everywhere except where they should be, then again didn't I use to be just like them? Hadn't

I, too, hankered for a celebrity to write about? Nor was Rolf able to get old colleagues to write about the postal directive, however, he did write quite a lot himself and published it on www.postdirektivet.no and one really beautiful day it was clear that eighteen of the TUC's twenty-five union leaders were willing to put their names to the op-ed and *Dagsavisen* was willing to print it. Rolf was proud of that and walked with ever more confident steps between our office and Møllergata 10, and one morning he knocked on my door looking really serious: 'It's done!'

For a moment I had feared he was serious in a bad way, but from his cheerful tone I gathered that was not the case.

'What is?'

'I'm a newly minted member of the Royal Norwegian Labour Party.'

'Oh! That's wonderful! Congratulations! How does it feel?'

'Not bad, not bad, mind you I can always cancel my membership.'

'How did you actually do it?'

'I made a phone call. They didn't ask for a character reference.'

'Just wait until they google you.'

'What do you mean?'

He looked so anxious that I started wondering what he was hiding which might be found on Google.

'I'm just joking, I'm messing with you,' I said, 'and now we only have one problem left.'

'Which is what?'

'Getting you an invitation to the annual party conference ball. I believe that's where it's all happening.'

'Well, that's your job.'

I took on the task as he had done his bit, and racked my brains to think of a woman who was single and so important to Labour, the government or the TUC that she would have been invited to the ball, but failed to think of any. I called the head of Postkom and explained the problem, he agreed that it would be good to have Rolf present in the actual function room and said he would see what he could do. A few days later he called to say he might have a solution.

'Go on!'

He had managed to get a copy of the guest list, but not found a lone woman he felt he could ask apart from Gerd-Liv Valla, who had already turned down the invitation. But a single, gay man, Helge Helseth, had offered to help. I thanked him, told him that was great news and asked him to keep it between ourselves.

I went to the window and leaned out. I closed my eyes and thought the air I inhaled came from other planets. Small things aren't always trifling, I thought, I opened my eyes and gazed at the treetops and the pretty maple leaves which were a luminous green and fluttering gently, and behind them were living and striving buildings that trusted the earth to carry them for a long time. Everything felt willing and almost friendly, and before I went to see Rolf, I checked again how

many people had signed the online petition and the elec-
tronic round-robin letter, several more with each day and on
this lovely day almost 12,000 in total. I knocked on his door
with the wonderful news and he grew taller in his chair; he
had written the final version of the round-robin letter when I
lost my ability to write PR. But how to publicise the numbers?
We called the head of Postkom who was as excited as we were
and in our excitement we decided to publish every single
name, to hell with the expense, all 12,000 of them, every
single one equally important, everyone must be included!
Rolf called *Dagsavisen* and booked the space, seven pages
in total, once that was done he leaned back in his reclining
leather chair and said that life as a PR consultant wasn't
that bad after all. I said I had a solution for the annual conference ball.

'Aha?'

'Helseth doesn't have a plus one.'

'Helseth?'

'A great regional delegate from Finnmark.'

'So I'll be going with her?'

'We'll add you as Helseth's plus one, but you can turn up
whenever you like and for the dinner you'll be seated next to a
woman, not Helseth, you know how it is, but should anyone
ask then say you're Helseth's plus one.'

'Helseth who?'

'I only remember Helseth, I'll look it up and get you the
full name in plenty of time.'

'In plenty of time? The ball is in five days.'

'Helseth doesn't matter, you don't even have to meet the person.'

'The person?'

'Have a good weekend, Rolf! Say hi to your wife from me!'

I felt something I would call anticipation. I was looking forward to Labour's annual party conference, it was unbelievable. I was looking forward to Rolf's op-ed being printed on Wednesday signed by eighteen trade union leaders, and the 12,000 names on Thursday. Though it was a shame that so few people read *Dagsavisen*, I didn't know anybody who did. But then again it was Postkom that had insisted on *Dagsavisen*, I reminded myself, and that was the most important thing. And other journalists would read *Dagsavisen*, that was the second most important thing. I bought *Dagsavisen* and sat on a bench in the sun in Palace Park while I looked forward to Wednesday and remembered an earlier walk in Palace Park when it wasn't sunny and I hadn't been feeling hopeful but anxious and troubled, as if I was on a ship seeking refuge on the shore yet not wanting to go ashore on the land I was looking for, and at the same time fearing I would never find a safe haven. But now I was looking forward to Labour's annual conference, if only this feeling would last!

Stein texted me to say he had Truls that weekend. He didn't mention my letter, nor was it the time or the place for it. I called Margrete and asked if it was OK if Truls, Stein's son, I said wondering if perhaps I'd never told her he had a son, came with us. She said it was fine, but also great that I let her know in advance so she had time to prepare. I wondered what she meant by prepare, perhaps she was referring to the food, I said he was only . . . then I couldn't remember how old he was or I didn't know, so instead I said he was young and didn't eat much. I texted Stein to say that Truls was very welcome indeed.

I left in plenty of time. I wanted to get there before Stein and Truls turned up so it wouldn't be awkward. My hands trembled on the steering wheel and I despaired at how little it took to rattle me. Every time I thought I had made some progress, I was back at square one. I tried to keep the insight I'd had in Palace Park at the forefront of my mind, but it grew harder the closer I got to Lommedalen. Margrete welcomed me in her apron and the suffocating world of my childhood caught up with me as the door opened. Mum was already there, she had stayed the night, Margrete said, I wondered how they had spent last night. I had been on my own reading my copy of EJ's letter to Helga Brun. I found it comforting that the words were the same every time. Repeating, rereading them didn't make them any less significant, quite the opposite. There was so much that was still opaque and blurred, but in that letter was something fixed, something that couldn't be changed, and yet in Margrete's hallway it slipped through my fingers. It wasn't her fault. She was a mere mortal who in addition to that was carrying another human being, and that was a miracle and a mystery, but there was no miracle or mystery in

Margrete's house, only Sunday paralysis. The furniture was new, new and modern, and yet it was faded, colourless, the flowers on the table wilting from lack of fresh air, I wilted in the stifling atmosphere, the rooms closed against the world, sealed off against the outside, just like when I was growing up, as if there was nothing of importance outside the four walls of our home, no open sky just a mass-produced horizon, no precipice, no struggle, no requirement other than to behave oneself, as if life's problems were all about keeping up appearances, as if all that mattered was to fall in line with every rule we ever came near. I entered Margrete's home, I was back in the home of my childhood and my throat tightened.

When the doorbell rang soon after I had hung up my coat, everyone knew it would be Stein and Truls. Margrete took off her apron, I couldn't tell anything from looking at her stomach, it was too early. I stood behind her while she opened the door, they had met a few times before, I remembered. Stein greeted her politely and introduced Truls. Truls stuck out his tiny hand. Stein hugged me and kissed me quickly on my neck, that was for the letter. They took off their shoes and hung up their coats and entered the living room with me, Mum got up from the sofa. And so she ended up greeting first Stein, then Truls and then me, we hugged one another and I could smell her apathy. Margrete asked if I could give her a hand in the kitchen and put on the apron again, I went with her.

'You haven't said anything about you know what, have you?' she whispered and I shook my head. She had put a large

162

wild salmon in the oven and would be serving it with potatoes and cucumber from a local farm in Lommedalen, for afters there was cloudberry cream pudding made with cloudberries from Hardangervidda.

'It's the real thing,' she said, taking off her apron and giving me the bowl with the potatoes, she took out the fish and we put them on the table, which was already laid.

'Lunch is served,' Margrete said in her hostess voice.

Now she's feeling confident again, I thought. Now she's back on firm ground, far from the precipice and the place she was when she rang me on Bygdøy and revealed a chink in her armour, something that had pleased me. Not because I wanted her to crack, but because her vulnerability had made her visible to me, she became audible to me with her hectic, too-quick voice too highly pitched, happy and terrified in one huge emotion for which there was no name. At the mercy of life's vagaries and the whims of nature, we can't control biology, no matter how real our food. But right now she felt confident and believed herself to be above life's vagaries and the whims of nature, how little it takes to move people from the edge of the precipice to believing that all good things come in threes.

'Think global, shop local,' she announced after reciting the menu in an almost didactic voice that sounded as if she was chastising someone, people who ate frozen pizzas, say, and I thought she was wasting her disapproval. And secondly, that it wasn't a call for action, but virtue signalling, a trendy façade.

Confident and in control, she stepped onto the stage, the most environmentally and allergy conscious of everyone in Lommedalen, she talked as if the simple answer to all of life's problems was better raw materials and it hurt to see that she liked herself better now, was more at ease with herself now than when she lost control and cracked. It's when we crack that we become lovable, I thought, like Stein cracked and I grew to love him and wrote him a letter and became happier. So did it follow that I, too, could show my insecurities and become lovable? Crack in front of them, here, now, in order to be loved?

'Have any of you heard about the postal directive?' I said.

There was no reaction. Trond asked me to pass him the potatoes and as I did, I looked him in the eye and asked specifically if he, Trond, had heard about the postal directive.

'No,' he said indifferently.

'Next week at its annual conference, the Labour Party will agree to adopt the postal directive,' I said, 'which will most probably mean the end of the standard delivery rate,' I said, 'and that will make it more expensive to send a letter from Drammen to Alta than from one end of Oslo to another.'

'A letter,' Margrete said, 'who sends letters these days?'

Stein looked up at me and smiled.

'Many of the things you need still arrive by post,' I said, 'bills, for example.'

She snorted with derision.

'Wouldn't you mind if you only got post five days a week?'

'Makes no difference to me.'

If I stopped now, it wouldn't count.

'I'm working to oppose the directive,' I said.

Stein was bent over Truls's plate, removing bones from the fish.

'You're always against everything,' Mum said.

There was an awkward silence just like when I was a child.

'Who's your client?' Stein said, coming to my rescue.

'Postkom. The Post and Communications Union.'

'You're working with a trade union? I didn't know that.'

'Me neither,' I said, 'it came about by chance.'

'Poor Truls,' Mum remarked, 'I don't think he likes fish.'

We looked at Truls who hadn't eaten much; she would appear to be right.

'Don't you like fish, Truls?'

Truls squirmed on his chair.

'You usually like fish, Truls,' Stein said before he realised his mistake because then it was just Margrete's wild salmon he didn't like.

'You don't have to clear your plate, Truls,' Mum said, Truls looked down.

'I hope you like cloudberry cream pudding,' Margrete said, Truls bowed his head even further and grew scarlet.

And that was the end of that, so much for being in the moment and revealing my insecurities. The miracle didn't happen, we were suspended in the mundane as if stuck in a bog and besides what on earth had made me think I could ever drag them out of it with a postal directive.

~

In the street outside Stein and I stood between our cars not knowing what to do, following my letter we had to talk to each other in a new way. It was still light because it was spring and there were wood anemones around a birch tree in a field across the road. Truls went to pick some.

'You're passionate about the postal directive,' Stein said.

'Yes, funny thing that,' I said.

'Why?'

'It's like it's become real for me. More real than ByggBo and especially the Real Thing.'

'What do you mean?'

'Well, that's what's so difficult to explain.'

'But you could try, couldn't you,' he said, 'after all, it's just me you're talking to.'

'Just you?' I said and laughed and he smiled and kissed me quickly and looked at Truls under the birch tree and kissed me for a long time. It was good to kiss outside in spring, it was a long time since I had done that.

I said it was about introducing competition for letters weighing less than 50g.

'Oh, come on,' he laughed, but I said it was a serious matter and explained the potential consequences and he understood and nodded and agreed and once the conversation was flowing I asked him if he got many letters. He rocked back and forth and said that he had just received one.

'I wasn't thinking of that one,' I said.

'You weren't?'

I said I was thinking of a letter which I had noticed he was so scared of me seeing in his flat once that he'd hidden it.

'Oh, that,' he said.

'What was it about?'

It was bold to ask him so directly, I hadn't planned to, but I had done it now and perhaps he was the person closest to me.

'It's embarrassing,' he said, looking down.

'Because?' I said, putting pressure on him, making it uncomfortable, and I was scared of the answer, scared of losing him just as I had realised I loved him, but something told me that the letter was crucial, just as crucial as the letter to Helga Brun, the way letters can be.

'The thing is, I'm not very good at communicating,' he began reluctantly, 'you could even say that I need a PR consultant.'

'Ha ha,' I said.

'No, really,' he said, 'sometimes when I don't know what to do,' he said, 'I'll write myself a letter.'

'Why? To support the Post Office?'

It was his turn to laugh.

'No,' he said, 'but when I express myself as if I'm not me, the words come to me,' he said, 'when I pretend I'm someone else, then I express myself more clearly and I send the letter to myself so I can see what I mean,' he said.

'Couldn't you just write the letter, put it away and then take it out another time?'

'I've tried that,' he said, 'but it's not the same. I have to do the whole thing, the envelope, the stamp, the post box, and then it really does work. It's about finding something that works.'

I knew exactly what he meant.

'So that letter you stuffed into your pocket so I wouldn't see it, that was from you to you?'

'Yes.'

He paused, then he looked down at me and said in a softer voice, 'And it said something about not letting you go, only much better put, of course, because it was expressed by the letter writer. As you can see, I'm my own PR consultant and quite a decent one really, all I cost is a few stamps every month, and if your postal directive isn't passed, the price won't go up.'

'That's by no means certain,' I said.

'Nothing is,' he said.

'True,' I said.

'But I believe that we're in the same place,' he said, 'that we have the same struggles. That we fail at the same things.'

Truls returned with wood anemones, Stein took them and before he got into the car, he bent down and whispered into my ear that he wished me every success with the Labour Party's annual conference and that he was looking forward to hearing all about it on Sunday.

I, too, was looking forward to it, I could feel, whatever the outcome. 'Read *Dagsavisen* on Wednesday! Read *Dagsavisen* on Thursday! Follow the Labour Party conference on the news!' I called out, 'it wouldn't surprise me if they mention the postal directive!'

That Wednesday the op-ed was printed in *Dagsavisen* under the headline 'Post and Profit' and with the subhead: 'We say no to taxpayer-funded liberalisation of the Postal Service. Use your right to object to the EU's postal directive!'

We were on the phone all day. Rolf had given me a list of names he and Thor Granengren had compiled in the late spring evenings over coffee and biscuits. Key Labour people who should be informed and reminded about the postal directive ahead of the annual conference. A woman from Hordaland who was fighting to save a local hospital, and a young woman from Buskerud who was fighting for the environment, and a man from Sogn og Fjordane who was fighting for a bridge to be built to a remote and windswept island. I felt very awkward when I rang the first person, but her reaction was positive and I stated my case concisely and reminded her how much anxious local patients depend on letters from the hospital arriving as safely and as quickly as possible, and the woman agreed with me. So I was less nervous when I called the next person and her reaction was also positive and I quickly stated my case and explained that if the postal directive was adopted and postal services became competitive, it would lead to many more half-empty post vans on the roads and more CO_2 in the atmosphere and the young woman said she hadn't thought of that, thanked me for the information and said that she would spread it around, so when I rang the third person, I felt encouraged by the first two and pledged my support for the bridge to the remote and windswept island which would ensure that the post would keep coming, as long as the postal directive wasn't adopted, because if it was then no one could guarantee that the post would reach the island by ferry or by car because it wouldn't be profitable. And the man from Sogn og Fjordane agreed with me completely and said he was good to go.

I continued making calls into the evening and had an epiphany like Rudolf Karena Hansen had when he started looking for Helga Brun. I gained an understanding of situations I previously hadn't known about, I heard stories about people I wouldn't otherwise have heard, I saw connections where I had never seen connections before, and I almost felt I belonged.

It wasn't until nine o'clock in the evening that I said goodbye to Rolf who stayed on. From the pavement I looked up at the light in his window next to Dag's office where there was no light. I saw Rolf pace up and down with the phone pressed against his ear and his left arm gesturing. I was very fond of him now. Perhaps we should celebrate Kraft-Kom's five-year anniversary after all? I didn't walk down to the multi-storey car park because I felt too full for my small car to contain me, I finally understood why we say full to bursting. Instead I walked the now familiar route to Møllergata 10 which was different at this time because it was evening and spring and people were out drinking, sitting under the city's heating lamps and smoking, and they seemed happy, but perhaps they dominated the scene because they were the ones who could afford to go out, and the junkies and the Romanian beggars had retreated to underneath the bridges and the small clusters of trees that were still left in the city. In Møllergata 10 the light was on in the office of the head of Postkom on the third floor, I positioned myself so I could get a better look, yes, there he was, pacing up and down like Rolf, his phone pressed against his ear and his left hand gesturing, it was a comforting sight. If I had kept a diary, I would have written about it. About the working human being, the committed human being, about people trying to change things, people investing their energy, talking to one another and coming together. And as I'd started walking, I decided to cross Youngstorget where I saw there was also activity in front of Folkets Hus Congress Centre, ladders and vans, men on the roof and on the façade; they, too, were preparing for tomorrow.

I didn't sleep that night, I tossed and turned anxiously although there was nothing to be anxious about. No one seriously believed the postal directive would be voted down, not even the head of Postkom. But he had to stay positive to spur himself on to fight until the bitter end, he owed his members that, he owed himself that, and he owed it to the cause. But was it worth the effort if we were doomed to fail? Was it nothing but an empty gesture? No, because our efforts would pay off, if not in the form of an outright victory, then in specific demands which the government would have to meet. This is politics, I said to myself in the car on my way there, my heart was pounding. I had learned a great deal about politics in recent months, I could have learned it sooner if I had spent more time talking to Dag, I thought, perhaps many things would have been different if Rolf, Dag and I had discussed politics in our breaks. My heart was beating so fast my hands trembled on the steering wheel, I stopped at the Kiwi shop but they didn't stock *Dagsavisen*, it didn't sell, my heart beat faster until I reached the Narvesen kiosk where they did stock it, I ran back to the car, scared to open it and find that it wasn't there, but it was, the petition and the 12,000 names, seven pages in total, it was wonderful! I turned on the radio to hear if they would mention it on the news, they didn't, I waited for the phone to ring, it didn't ring, I tuned the car radio to P4 to distract myself until I saw Rolf, Abba's 'money-money-money' thumped towards me and I drummed my hands against the steering wheel and rocked back and forth, parked in the multi-storey car park and ran upstairs, Rolf had showered, he wore a freshly ironed shirt, his hands were restless and his eyes were blazing, on his desk *Dagsavisen* lay open on the petition pages: 'Are you ready?'

I nodded, we half-ran to Møllergata, we raced up the stairs, unable to wait for the slow lift, the door to the office of the head of Postkom was open, three staff members were inside bent over *Dagsavisen*, when the head of Postkom saw us he turfed them out brusquely, I had never seen him brusque before, and a solemn mood descended.

We went through our programme for the day. We had a plan A and we had a plan B. Who would talk to who. Who had yet to make up their minds, who might change their minds and on what conditions. We had reviewed our plans before, but now everything was in motion, unpredictable, we sharpened our knives, donned our armour, stiffened our sinews, I told my heart to settle down, my digestion to ease up, my blood to run more smoothly, I ordered all of the noisy, complicated machinery that was me to fall silent so the others wouldn't realise the true state I was in. We shook hands, wished each other luck and silently made our way to Youngstorget, to the battlefield.

We could see from afar that it was buzzing with activity outside Folkets Hus Congress Centre. Big banners with 'Labour Party 2011 Annual Conference' flapped in the spring breeze, a line of flags, a mixture of Labour Party and Norwegian ones, had been hoisted on the roof and big posters of Prime Minister Jens Stoltenberg festooned the entrance, there were people everywhere. As we got closer to the colourful spectacle, we were approached by postal workers who were Labour members, handing out flyers opposing the postal directive and we took them with encouraging comments. Keep up the good work! Well done! They had been told to keep a distance of twenty metres from the main entrance by

173

Raymond Johansen, Labour's general secretary, who was strictly enforcing the ban on the distribution of anything that might come across as propaganda. We had applied for permission to distribute the Postkom members newsletter to the delegates, but been refused. The Oslo branch of Labour wasn't even allowed to hand out disposable toothbrushes left over from the last general election, because there would be a vote on state payment for dental care at this year's conference. The postal workers who were Labour members respected the twenty metres zone, but if they saw someone they believed to be a delegate head for the entrance, they would run to intercept them with a flyer before they reached the exclusion zone. Rolf and I followed close at the heels of the head of Postkom as he made his way through the crowds, greeting people left right and centre, chatting to anyone he thought might be useful about the postal directive, a dozen or so conversations from the steps to the registration desk, the head of Postkom was an official guest, Rolf was attending in his capacity as a regular party member, he whispered to me that he hoped they wouldn't check whether his commitment was genuine. He met fellow journalists from his time before Kraft-Kom, the head of Postkom knew everyone, I was the only one without a badge, I felt excluded and alien, I didn't know the language, couldn't read the codes, I stood on my own, my gaze fixed on the back of the head of Postkom, feeling sorry for myself and crushed by my old sense of isolation in the middle of a crowd when I bumped into my old school friend from the Metro and had to admit that it was me. To be real and be present in the now, that is the question, and it didn't depend on which group I happened to be in or outside, I mustn't forget that! People began milling into the conference hall, there had to be at least a thousand, I positioned myself so that I could see the head of Postkom sit down on the VIP bench with the other trade union leaders, Rolf took one of the seats for regular members behind the press corps, the doors closed and I was outside. I would be reporting from outside, but outside is also an important place from which to report.

Soon I heard Abba music, not 'money-money-money' but something similar, Rolf was texting on his iPhone that two actors from the Christian Ringnes Theatre production of *Mamma Mia* would be the cultural feature. After Abba they sang something about light and warmth, he texted, I stayed as close to the door as I dared without alerting the security guards. Rolf texted that the prime minister had started his opening address by honouring prominent party members who had passed away since the last conference, he couldn't possibly mention them all. Nor did he mention the postal directive, Rolf texted, I sat with *Dagsavisen* opened on the petition, having decided to read every single one of the 12,000 names and I took out a subscription seeing as I was there, I told Rolf during a break, he blushed and told me he had done likewise. Many people were mentioning the postal directive, he told me, and after a while the head of Postkom came out and said that many speakers had opposed the postal directive and had been applauded when they spoke out against it and that other speakers had started throwing in an 'incidentally, I'm against the postal directive too' irrespective of their supposed topic, simply to get a round of applause. I had made myself comfortable in a seating area in a corner and taken out my laptop, got myself some coffee, been to the lavatory a couple of times and was starting to feel at home, it doesn't take much. We humans are very good at adapting, I thought, by no means an original observation, but it didn't matter because people mimic one another and I finally realised what it meant to adapt and I felt a sense of belonging by thinking and expressing what others have thought and expressed. Rolf worked on the reporters who were there and tried to convince them that the postal directive was a cause the party leadership could lose, but no one believed him. The leadership will gallop through the items on the agenda, was the refrain, no surprise there, it was our refrain too. But not before we've put pressure on them and obtained some concessions, Rolf declared, but concessions and compromises didn't make for very interesting news coverage.

The head of Postkom was in one section of the hall, but mostly outside it in order to get an idea of who would be speaking on the postal directive. Whenever someone did, he would rush back in and soon came out again to report back, and I made notes. But even when he and Rolf were both in the hall I would occasionally overhear something as I sat, apparently all innocence, behind *Dagsavisen* having got as far as the signatories whose surnames started with B, when what I was really doing was eavesdropping on a conversation between the delegates from Telemark. They were discussing a Real

Madrid vs Barcelona match. But the subject of the postal directive also came up, I heard because it was discussed in loud and angry tones, even passionate EU supporters were against it, and I reported that when my colleagues came out in the breaks, they nodded, they too had noticed that.

When that day's session ended at nine thirty in the evening, we headed to Santinos, an Italian restaurant nearby, for pizza. Rolf handed me his phone and said he had saved the best till last.

The sounds in the background were the sounds I heard every time the big doors opened. The sound of many people and whooshing microphones and scrambling chair legs, footsteps and a hum of voices, clapping and shouting and whispering, but also an expectant silence whenever the speakers stepped up to the lectern in front of the red wall with Labour's famous slogan We're All in This Together. The floor was given to a delegate from Hordaland, a young dark-haired man who strode onto the podium and, with an enviable conviction in his voice, he leaned forwards eagerly because what he had to say was so heartfelt and serious and meant so much to him, he was sincere, his commitment was huge as was his determination to contradict the party leadership, which only those who know they have a strong cause possess. People move away from the districts for many reasons, he began. You can't get a decent soy latte for a start, he said cheerfully before getting to the crux of his argument. Vibrant, local communities don't just happen, he said, holding up the government's own commissioned research. It made sombre reading for a social democrat, he said. The postal directive is a European race to the bottom in social dumping, he said, and added that full-time German postal workers now earned so little money they were forced to apply for benefits in order to make ends meet. He was pro-EU, he said, but he was also aware that the EU had a Conservative majority. That the proposal to make postal services competitive had come up before, but back then the Norwegian Labour Party had said no. And what the EU wanted to introduce now was to all intents and purposes the same thing. Should Norway adopt a policy it didn't want and that would cost billions? Use taxpayers' money to keep the Post Office afloat while commercial players in Østlandet grew rich? Everything I had thought, had tried to articulate, that Rolf had tried to articulate, but which had remained anaemic, including the op-ed in *Dagsavisen*, here it was. If I may quote the King, he said: Return to sender! It was simple, primitive in the best, most basic sense of the word. 'Now the woods awaken,' he quoted finally, 'now the fields arise. It's the hour of creation, but never compromise!'

We sat in silence after watching it. And for a long time with no thoughts about tomorrow, although tomorrow was a crucial day.

I wished that Dag could have seen it, it was the kind of moment that changes everything, that changes lives. A young person taking to the podium, having his say, stating his opinion, speaking truth to power because he's in touch with the grassroots; it means that those who hear him understand there's a way out, and not the one Dag took.

That night I dreamed Dag was sitting in his chair. I turned up at the office and there was Dag in his chair, slumped and apathetic, his arms dangling over the armrests, his hands limp against the floor. His head lolled, toothless, his face was covered in tears the size of pearls, when he saw me he got up and staggered outside as though he was drunk or ill. It was snowing heavily, I wondered how the woefully underdressed Dag would manage in the snow, soon it would reach up to the window, cover the window, I wanted to open the door, but I couldn't, I was snowed in and could see nothing but the office because of the snow outside, the city was covered in snow, perhaps another ice age had arrived and it might last a hundred years. Soon there was rumbling, the building started to tremble, it's collapsing under the snow, I thought, the room shuddered and I felt dizzy, when the shaking finally stopped, the room was tilting and all the furniture had careered down to the other end; there was a truck wheel in the snow outside, a truck had come off the icy road, it had crashed into a pile of snow and been broken up into its individual parts and one heavy wheel had landed in front of my window and behind the wheel a strange flower grew from the snow, which lay fine and white and would be great for skiing outside my window where the sun was now shining.

~

We met in Møllergata the next morning to discuss strategy. Most of the items on today's agenda didn't relate to the postal directive, it was the prime minister's summing up at twenty past eleven that interested us. But still it was important to be present, plead our case, argue, convince, encourage. Report, I added in my quiet and now slightly less tense mind. It felt easier to walk up the steps today, some people nodded, I settled down in the same corner with a copy of every single newspaper to look for coverage of the directive. Rolf and the head of Postkom entered the hall, but Rolf soon returned, he had started smoking, he whispered to me that if it hadn't been for the postal directive he would have cancelled his Labour membership immediately, proceedings were that dull and predictable.

'And when it's dull, but you're excited then it's almost unbearable,' he said. He carried Thor Granengren's list in his inside pocket, he kept going behind a pillar to study the now grubby and dog-eared list, staring hard at the delegates' name badges to check if he was facing an important member before he launched into his spiel, spending more and more time out on the steps in the spring weather with a Marlboro Light in his mouth beneath the big poster of the prime minister and with a view of Youngstorget, eagerly discussing the postal directive with other smokers. At a quarter past eleven, he stubbed out his cigarette and came inside. I was outside the door to the conference hall as close as I dared to the security guards.

~

The prime minister announced that he was aware of strong opposition to the postal directive. He said – in a voice that betrayed how much he dreaded turning up in Brussels with a result that signalled his impotence within his own party – that the main thing was to get support for the political principle. Several of the demands made in connection with the directive could be met without the need for a veto. The government was willing to guarantee that the same postage charges would apply across all of Norway and that the six-day delivery service would continue.

'What did I tell you,' Rolf whispered to the reporters, but they didn't think the guarantees were newsworthy.

'Trust us,' the prime minister said by way of conclusion. Some people clapped.

The resolutions committee got to work.

Rolf hung around and heard that several county branches refused to change their minds despite the prime minister's commanding speech, I made notes. The head of Postkom stayed at his post on the VIP bench, texting us to say several speakers had mentioned the importance of stopping the postal directive while debating local government issues.

'Local government issues?' I said.

'That's what I'm telling you,' Rolf said.

The head of Postkom came out, he was agitated, he'd heard that several members of the resolutions committee were willing to go against the party line and issue a statement against the directive! The activity in the foyer rose notably, people whispered in hushed voices, mobile phones beeped constantly.

'They're beginning to see that they might lose,' the head of Postkom said, pointing to the aides and party staff who had been sent out from on high to talk to local government leaders and get them to toe the line. If you do this, then we'll do that, and if you don't then x, y and z, and local government here, postal directive there, and support for this that and the other. The county delegates who had come mandated, but especially those who hadn't, were singled out by the messengers of the mighty and asked to flip and were leaned on to flip, while Rolf and the head of Postkom gave the very same people our pep talk, focussing especially on members of Young Labour, who had yet to be case-hardened, yet to become opportunistic, yet to be disillusioned in terms of what was possible and what wasn't. 'Steady, solid and strong opposition!' the head of Postkom chanted, but added that it was a tough job to oppose the postal directive when you were up against a resolutions committee of experienced players and mightily led by Church Minister Rigmor Aasrud, who was prepared to bend over backwards to accommodate demands in order to avoid a veto. That's how it's usually done, the head of Postkom said. You promise small things in order to get the big ones through, buttons and glass beads in return for principles. Because power is like an elephant, he said, it may be hard to describe, but you'll know it when you see it. There were many elephants in Folkets Hus Congress Centre these days, I understood, some real heavyweights, I recognised them from the newspapers and the television, and even more of medium size, I didn't know who they were, but the head of Postkom pointed them out to me. And quite a few little ones who were looking forward to becoming big ones in time. The head of Postkom himself was an elephant and knew the language of the elephants. But there was another language that was equally necessary, one which had sustained me these last few months. It was the language spoken in the shadows and in the corners and on remote islands and in seedy dives and in attics, in bedrooms and letters and on the phone by those standing at the edge of the precipice and those who are falling. A language that has no agenda other than to express a truth about the writer, just like the postal worker had written plainly that he hoped the years wouldn't be tough. A language that didn't seek to spin or obfuscate, but to open and elevate, a language that had helped me to greater clarity, which had pulled me from the mire. And that language had to be preserved and protected because without it no one would survive, including the elephants. Because elephants, too, dream of not being elephants and yearn for something higher which can't be described with or advertised in elephant language.

I made up my mind to buy myself a diary and cultivate that language.

We were there until nine thirty that evening as well, then had a brief meeting in the foyer before we each went our separate ways, I went home, Rolf went home, so I thought, but he rang me from Justisen Bar at eleven thirty. There he had been buttonholed by an agitated aide to the foreign minister who claimed it was irresponsible to veto the postal directive at this stage. The reasonable, democratic and responsible choice would be to make some demands now and then use the right of veto later if those demands weren't met.

'But that's what's going to happen,' Rolf said he had replied, and now he said it again, 'that's what's going to happen.'

I was there at nine o'clock the next morning as agreed, Rolf didn't show. I rang him, he didn't answer his phone. The head of Postkom was inside the conference hall, I sat alone missing Rolf, it was a strange feeling. We're business partners, I thought, and it was good to remember that and it was good to see him when he turned up just before ten o'clock, his voice rusty.

'My wife found out I've started smoking,' he mumbled, 'but I've negotiated a compromise. I'll smoke for the duration of the party conference and then I'll stop!'

He slipped inside, but soon reappeared because they were debating local government issues and he needed a cigarette. The head of Postkom was also hanging around outside, trying to find out how the postal directive was progressing in the resolutions committee and within local government.

'Look,' he whispered, pointing to how one local government leader after another was dragged into meetings with Støre, Stoltenberg and Johansen.

'The grassroots are on our side, they're having to do their dirty work themselves!'

The day finished early, the hall needed setting up for tonight's ball.

'This Helseth,' Rolf wanted to know, 'should I go say hello to her?'

'You don't have to arrive together,' I said, 'you just tell them that you're Helseth's plus one on the door, you're on the guest list.'

'I know, but even so.'

'The head of Postkom has checked, you'll be seated next to a lovely delegate from Nordland at the dinner. Why don't we have a beer,' I said, we went to Santinos as we had done the other night. When he had drunk half his beer, I told him.

'His name is Helge.'

'Who?'

'Your plus one.'

'Eh?'

'Helge Helseth.'

'Come again?'

'You don't even need to meet him, on the door just say that you're Helge's plus one, you don't even have to mention his first name, just say Helseth.'

'But people will think I'm gay!'

'Oh, for God's sake and what if they do? Do you have a problem with gay people?'

'No, no, but really, Ellinor.'

'You don't have to go to the ball, it's up to you, but if you want to get in, your only option is to be Helge's plus one. By the way, he's a good-looking guy.'

'Have you met him?'

'No, but he's against the postal directive.'

'Right, right.'

He drained his glass.

'OK, then,' he said.

'The resolutions committee is working flat out right now,' I said.

He nodded pensively.

'OK, then,' he said again and ordered another beer, I had one too, I decided to leave the car, it was a special occasion.

'But you'll come with me,' he said, 'you promise to wait, to be there?'

It warmed the cockles of my heart, as they say.

'Of course,' I said, 'after all, we're business partners!'

We went to the office where he changed from a grey to a black suit and then to Folkets Hus where people in festive clothes were queueing up on the steps to the entrance, ladies in long dresses and men in suits and a very excited head of Postkom, who told us that the resolutions committee hadn't yet finished. One person was still dissenting, the deputy leader of Young Labour.

Poor deputy leader, we sighed, and though I stood out in my daytime clothes I, too, was offered an aperitif and we raised our glasses to toast the deputy leader of Young Labour who so bravely stood her ground for our cause.

'Have you met Helge Helseth?' the head of Postkom said, introducing an ageing man missing several teeth. Rolf paled, but I greeted Helseth, who was a conference delegate from Finnmark and knew Rudolf Karena Hansen well. Rolf went off to track down the delegate from Nordland, soon everyone had gone inside the conference hall and I was almost alone, but before long more people came outside to smoke and gossip and speculate and many mentioned the postal directive. I sat in a cubicle in the ladies' lavatory listening to women expressing despair and outrage at the party's leadership who kept bringing people in to put pressure on them regarding the directive, and Rolf texted me about how the party leadership kept dragging people aside to get them to change their minds about the directive, the delegate from Nordland had noticed it as well. And I replied that I was well aware of it because in the Ladies they spoke of little else. Rolf finally came out at eleven thirty, we were standing on the steps when a member of the resolutions committee came up to bum a cigarette and told us when he got a light that the resolutions committee had finished its work and that the majority had agreed an excellent statement on the postal directive, he clearly had no idea who we were. Rolf tried to wheedle the details out of him, but he refused, Rolf then demanded that the head of Postkom be shown the statement, the man looked doubtful. Or else, Rolf said and clenched his fists and the man agreed. Rolf fetched the head of Postkom, who was taken to the back room to meet with Raymond Johansen, Labour's general secretary, and Rigmor Aasrud, twenty minutes later he came back, ashen-faced. The statement met every single demand Postkom had made, what do we do now? After all, the aim wasn't to stop the directive just for the sake of it, he said. The aim was to gain support for the political principle, he said, sounding as if he was quoting someone, though it didn't make it any less true if he were.

We looked at one another, we were exhausted.

'Well, we seem to have achieved our goal,' the head of Postkom said wearily, he wasn't quite himself after his brush with power.

'It's more than we could have hoped for,' the head of Postkom said, he was trying to look on the bright side.

Others joined us, heard about the statement and remarked: 'Support for everything? Well done!'

And so the head of Postkom slunk back to Raymond Johansen and Rigmor Aasrud and accepted the statement with a few minor changes. A long day's journey into night was over for most people, but not for us. The Three Musketeers shuffled down to Møllergata 10 to discuss the consequences. The head of Postkom got a text message telling him Young Labour was pissed off with us and that hurt, but we did understand that Young Labour was disappointed that Postkom had ultimately caved under massive pressure. But still it was a victory of sorts, we had to bear that in mind! Because if those concessions were granted, the EU wouldn't accept them and we could use our right of veto after all! We kept repeating that! The government hadn't won support for anything other than starting the process, which the EFTA agreement sketched out, for disputes between the parties, we said as we sat there, dispirited and not feeling terribly proud of ourselves. Exactly, we said and nodded tellingly. And so we tried to convince ourselves, console ourselves, talk our disappointment and our broken dream into victory. History is written by the victors, but defeated PR consultants contribute. It wasn't until two o'clock in the morning that we took a cab home and Rolf drafted a press release in which Postkom expressed satisfaction with the statement from the resolutions committee.

Sunday morning I felt very tired, but I had to get up even earlier than the previous days, the press release had to be ready at a quarter past eight. I took a cab rather than the Metro, which ran few trains on Sundays, it was an emergency. At seven thirty I turned up in Møllergata where the head of Postkom told me that Young Labour had also withdrawn their opposition during the night, we could easily imagine how that had happened. The resolution was thus unanimous and I was pleased about that because I didn't like Young Labour being upset and it probably meant that the resolution was good enough and would also be good enough for Rudolf Karena Hansen and Asfrid Basso and the other people from the media training course who had been on my mind while I couldn't sleep.

We polished the press release, printed it out, made copies and went to Folkets Hus where we distributed them to the press and gave a copy to Raymond Johansen, who came by and liked the wording so much that he made sure it was copied and distributed to everyone.

Rolf, the head of Postkom and others entered the conference hall. I took a seat in the chair, which had become mine, to see what the newspapers were writing about the postal directive – not a lot, as it turned out. And anyway it made no difference now, the matter had been decided, and I couldn't help dreading and worrying about tomorrow when there would be no postal directive. We had a few summing-up meetings, were due to write a brief report and then say our goodbyes to the head of Postkom, the postal directive and Møllergata 10 before we went back to our office and Dag's empty desk. Back to writing for the Real Thing or something equally pointless, to being an empty barrel who rumbled to make a living. I was overwhelmed by despair and thoughts of tomorrow, I abandoned my laptop and mobile and ran outside, past the crowds on the steps, I couldn't bear their sounds, their chatting, their gossiping, their camaraderie, their wheeler-dealering; you're just tired, I tried telling myself, you're just worn out, I justified myself, but couldn't stand my own inner critic, I ran until I could taste blood in my mouth to the grassy area by Kirkeristen, flung myself down on it, buried my face in it, sobbed into it and recalled my recent dream. I immersed myself in it, the big truck wheel outside the window, the wheel of life and the strange flower and finally the sun, I lost myself in it and slowly I calmed down and began to sense how I belonged to the earth and when I opened my eyes, I saw a huge yellow dandelion growing right behind a bush and it looked joyful, or so it seemed to me, because it grew behind a bush and was a dandelion and yellow. And I got up, dusted myself down and calmly walked back while I thought about Rudolf Karena Hansen's 'life or death' with every step, with every decision, on which side would I stand? I had a choice and I had to choose, we all had to, so would it be ice age or spring? I could give up the Real Thing, all it took was one keystroke, one sentence, give it up in order to give myself to something else, it's never too late to start. I thought I'd understood that, but certain things, I realised now, must be understood over and over again. My breathing was settling down and we had won our concessions, I reminded myself, so Norwegian postal workers wouldn't have to endure the same conditions as the German ones, God help them, and yes, it was a dangerous trend across the world, but in that case I must make my contribution, step up to the podium, show my face rather than hide away, depressed and repressed, because my apathy was one of the reasons why the number of things I couldn't stand was growing. It's never too late to start, I repeated to myself as if building up to a speech because these simple words opened rather closed, they inspired hope of change, and as long as there's hope there's life in your life, I said to myself as I walked up the steps to Folkets Hus and over to my corner where no one had stolen my laptop or my mobile, something of a miracle in itself given how many people were there. Rolf had texted me to say that Rigmor Aasrud had presented the resolution so it could be voted through when the time came, and the time soon came because it had grown late while I had been out finding myself. Rolf then texted that the time was now, but that a young woman from Akershus was speaking to second a motion from Rogaland to reject the postal directive. The postal directive had been a central issue at the annual party conference, she said, so the conference ought to have its say. Besides, she was angry at how the party leadership had shamelessly tried to influence the party's highest body in an undignified, reprehensible and underhand way and had spoiled the ball for everyone!

The hall erupted in applause, Rolf wrote, I heard it, and people hadn't stopped clapping when a middle-aged woman from Rogaland took the floor and said that the last speaker had her full support and that she was even angrier with the party leadership for putting pressure on people and behaving in an embarrassing way, and especially for ruining the ball. It hadn't been as much fun as it usually was! More applause followed, then it was time to vote, and the motion from Rogaland to reject the postal directive was passed by 181 out of 300 votes, it was incredible.

I had stood up, the people around me had stood up, we heard the uproar coming from the conference hall, it was like an earthquake, the building was trembling, there was stomping, clapping, shouting, whistling, cheering, it was historic, it had never happened before and no one had ever thought that it could happen, and the party leadership blanched and looked rattled and couldn't believe their own ears and eyes, and the doors opened and I saw whooping, standing people wave their arms in the air and Rolf came out, he was euphoric: 'Did you see that? Did you see that?' No, I didn't see it, but I heard it, you couldn't miss it, the journalists made a beeline for the head of Postkom, who struggled to string a sentence together because he was so overcome with emotion and the news was on everyone's lips and on the Internet. There was tweeting, hugging, embracing and in the hysteria and the happy confusion that ensued, I slipped into the conference hall and gathered up all the press releases we had handed out that morning and amended them so that 'Postkom content with postal directive resolution' now read 'Postkom VERY content with postal directive resolution'.

Rolf organised the many reporters who were clamouring to talk to the head of Postkom, reporters from television, radio and the newspapers. The foreign minister will have to go to Brussels after being defeated at home, the foreign minister will have to go to Brussels with a 'no' in his pocket. NRK and *Aftenposten* wanted to interview the head of Postkom at the main Post Office building in Lørenskog, we took a taxi there, anything for the press. Stein called to congratulate us and said he looked forward to hearing about it all.

If only Dag could have seen this, I thought, and regretted his untimely death.

Møllergata 10 on 10 April, it's five in the afternoon. We have opened the windows to let spring in, we have opened bottles of wine. We are many, Postkom employees and postal workers who have put off their flights home to be here and savour this, prolong this. We recount the events. We retell the story of last night's disappointment, we relive our doubts and exhaustion before we recapture our joy. If we need to, we can repeat this joy in our minds and our hearts. It doesn't mean much in the greater scheme of things, of course not, it's just a postal directive. One small step for Labour's grassroots, but a life-changing one for me because through working on the postal directive, I had learned the value of this step for living well and in good spirits. I knew now that no one is insignificant and that every day every one of us must choose whether to build civilisation or the opposite, let the world fall apart, and that even the smallest things present each of us with a challenge.

Stein picked me up around six o'clock. I hugged Rolf yet again, I hugged the head of Postkom, I hugged random people, I hugged Stein when he turned up, he had brought food and wine and wanted to hear everything. And I told him to the best of my ability what I thought was the beginning of my small, one-woman revolution.

It began the day I found my old diary. Or maybe it was the day Dag left. When he quit so spectacularly. When he showed me that it was possible to do something drastic, to quit, and I understood that I, too, wanted to do something drastic, to quit. Or perhaps it was the day Dag died, when he took irreversible action to kill himself. It had been an ordinary day. I had got up as usual, made coffee, turned on my computer and started work on ByggBo. Then Rolf rang and asked me to come to the office, then we learned that Dag had quit, and later that Dag had died, and I, too, was dead somehow yet still living, and in order to stay alive I had to do something.

It was the morning of 11 April 2011. I heard the papers arrive and went to pick up *Aftenposten* as always and *Dagsavisen* and also, to complete the set, *Klassekampen*, even if I hadn't quite reached the point of being willing to sell it on the street, at least I had it delivered to my door, and all three of them covered the postal directive extensively and the PM and the foreign minister looked utterly miserable in every single picture.

I went for a walk in the spring morning, pleasantly giddy from lack of sleep and with all my senses heightened. I could hear birds sing above me and see wood anemones in the verges below me, they didn't worry about tomorrow, nor did I want to trouble this wonderful day with tomorrow although I knew that tomorrow would come and bring its own challenges.

When tomorrow came as expected, I bought a diary and some elegant, cream-coloured cards. I wrote to Rudolf Karena Hansen to congratulate him on the victory. I wrote to Rolf to thank him for our happy collaboration and to say how much I'd enjoyed working with him on this project, I wanted to write and thank so many people when I heard the postman in the stairwell. I waited by my door in anticipation until he had gone. Then I ran down with my key. There was rarely anything in my letter box, but you never can tell. Behind the telephone bill was an envelope with my name in crooked capitals like those written by a child. I went back upstairs before I opened it. It was a letter from Truls. He thanked me for the Postman Pat book and wrote that he had decided to become a postman when he grew up. I sat down immediately to thank him for his thank you letter and wrote that I thought his was a bold choice. I added that it's important to choose boldly in big as well as in little things. Then I opened my diary.